# London's river tales for Children

Illustrated by
Belinda Evans

# London's river tales for Children

## Anne Johnson
## and Sef Townsend

The History Press

First published 2022

The History Press
97 St George's Place, Cheltenham,
Gloucestershire, GL50 3QB
www.thehistorypress.co.uk

British Library Cataloguing in Publication Data.
A catalogue record for this book is available from the British Library.

ISBN 978 0 7509 9561 0

Typesetting and origination by The History Press
Printed and bound in Great Britain by TJ Books Limited, Padstow, Cornwall.

Trees for LYfe

About the Authors and Illustrator 8

Introduction: The Many Rivers of London
and Their Stories 10

*Old Father Thames* 25

1 The Lion Keeper's Apprentice 27

2 Grace O'Malley: The Girl Who Became
a Pirate 42

*A Full Moon* 57

3 Mary Godwin: A Childhood by the
River Fleet 59

4 Frost Fairs on the Frozen River Thames 71

5 A Near Escape 86

*Dark River* 99

6 Safe at Last: Refugees on the Wandle 102

*Spring to Stream – What's in a Name?* 118

7 The Silver Darlings 121

8 Greenland on the Thames 133

*Sailor Talk* 150

9 From Riverbed to Barge 152

*The Riverbed* 166

10 Ferries and Fishes 168

*A Boat by Any Other Name* 179

11 The Whale Road 181

*Old Norse* 189

The
Many
Rivers of
London

Westbo

Ful

Richmond

Rive
Wand

Kingston

# ABOUT THE AUTHORS AND ILLUSTRATOR

ANNE JOHNSON was born on Canvey Island in the Thames Estuary and now lives by the Thames in Deptford. She is a writer, songwriter and storyteller and the Director of Everyday Magic, a London based charity that, for the last eighteen years, has been bringing live storytelling and music into schools.

SEF TOWNSEND has been a Londoner for more than forty years and much of that time he has spent living by the river. He tells traditional tales collected on his many travels around the world, where he works with children and adults, who are always keen to hear stories of London and its rivers.

BELINDA EVANS has been creating images for illustration, greetings cards and calendars for many years. She's always been lucky enough to live near a river, first in a flat overlooking the Thames at Greenwich, then in a house built above an underground section of the River Effra overflow. Now she's moved again and enjoys daily walks along the River Ravensbourne.

# INTRODUCTION

# THE MANY RIVERS OF LONDON AND THEIR STORIES

When we talk about London, most people know about the River Thames. The Thames is London's big river. But did you know that there are actually twenty-one rivers in London apart from the Thames? Many of them have been forced underground by the development of the city but they all have their own history and their own stories to tell.

# The River Thames

Although it is only tiny in comparison to the Amazon, the Nile or the Congo, the Thames has been known, for hundreds of years, as one of the greatest rivers of the world – just like them. It has been England's main waterway since the time of the Romans, who named it *Thamesis* and built the first city of *Londinium* on its banks.

By the time the new St Paul's Cathedral was built after the Great Fire of London, the Thames had become one of the world's busiest rivers and there were so many ships along it that there were traffic jams – or river jams. By then, London had become the biggest city in Europe, with ships leaving for and arriving from everywhere around the globe, bringing new goods and people here. The very first coffee, cocoa, tomatoes, bananas and exotic spices arrived up the Thames to be taken all around the country for people to try out these strange new foods. Immigrants, refugees and, very sadly, slaves too, arrived here as London became the centre of the huge British Empire. You will read some of their stories in the pages that follow.

Some of the most important events in British history happened on the banks of the Thames – such as the plot to blow up the Houses of Parliament, the Great Plague and the Great Fire of London. Important prisoners were taken by boat down the river

to be put into the scary Tower of London, from where they might never have left. Royal palaces were built on the riverbanks and in one of them Queen Elizabeth I entertained a strange pirate guest, who you can read about in one of the stories. There were pageants, or water parties, on the Thames where the King would sail down the river, lying back on luxurious red velvet couches while many boats with his important guests followed behind, listening to the music played by floating orchestras, entertained by fireworks and eating banquets of the finest food.

But, of course, some of the important events were not always such fun. Some children, called mudlarks, had to earn their living by searching in the mud for anything valuable that might have been dropped from a ship. The river sometimes turned violent and a surge of water from the North Sea would sweep upstream and flood many people out of their homes. You'll read that, thankfully, this doesn't happen anymore because of the Thames Barrier.

Another tale will take us back to the time when the Thames often froze over in the winter. This led to the Frost Fairs, when a tent city would be set up on the river with amusements, food and winter games.

There are also stories about fish in the Thames. But fishing on the river came to an end in the middle of Queen Victoria's reign. So much dirt and sewage were going into the Thames that it became dangerous even to breathe in the fumes from the river. This became known as the 'Great Stink'. People became ill, the fish died, the river was declared 'dead' and the politicians in Parliament couldn't work because, being right next to the river, they were choking. That led to huge

sewers being built, which helped, but it is only in the last fifty years that the river has really been cleaned up. Now life has returned to the 'dead' water and the good news is that the fish are back! An amazing 125 different kinds of fish can be found today in London's biggest river.

## Some of the Other Rivers of London

The other, smaller London rivers also have many stories to tell. Along them people were able to bring in grain to make flour and hay to feed their animals, especially all the horses needed for transport. They were able to build water mills and provide fresh drinking water for people when the River Thames itself had become too dirty to drink. Some, like the Wandle, Lea and Ravensbourne, still splash along and flow above ground, but the ones known as the 'lost rivers', because they are now underground, are still flowing beneath the streets and thoroughfares of London.

And they all had roles to play in making London the biggest capital city of Europe. In fact, one of the most important rivers in the world is here in London and most people have never even heard of it. That's probably because if you take the Waterloo and City Line underground train or walk into the great Bank of England, you wouldn't know that underneath you there is a river flowing down to the Thames. So, let's start with this one …

### *The River Walbrook*

It was one of the most important rivers in the world – and you've probably never heard of it! Although it is a very small river, and one that disappeared underground many years ago, without the Walbrook there wouldn't be a London as we know it today. It was this river that helped the Romans to find a place to build the city's first port, *Londinium*. They could defend it easily and safely harbour their ships, bringing all the goods from the Roman Empire. Most importantly, the

Walbrook gave the people plenty of fresh water to drink.

The new Roman invaders could build the first strong city between the two hills, Ludgate Hill (where St Paul's Cathedral now stands) and Cornhill, on either side of this little, but important, river. For the first time in England, there were brick and stone buildings with underfloor heating, public baths, shops and theatres, all with beautiful mosaics in the floor. And the Romans built their temple to the god Mithras. From the River Walbrook the Romans spread out over most of Britain, stayed for 500 years and found the perfect spot to build *Londinium*, where the Walbrook and the Thames come together.

### *The River Lea*

Unlike the Walbrook, the River Lea is much longer. Grain was brought down the river from the countryside outside London so that the people on the north side of the

Thames could grind it into flour for their bread. Hay was also brought along the river to feed the horses and donkeys who had to pull the carts and carriages that took people and goods around the city, in the days before cars and lorries.

During the Great Plague of London in 1665–66, the river became famous when bargemen from the town of Ware brought fresh water and food in their sailing barges for the people trapped in the city. The heroic bargemen were awarded the Freedom of the River Thames by the grateful citizens of London. This meant that, unlike others who sailed into London, they never had to pay taxes for using the city's waters.

One hundred and fifty years later, the River Lea became famous again when gunpowder from the Royal Gunpowder Mill at Waltham Abbey was transported down to the Thames and the waiting ships. The gunpowder played its role in winning the Battle of Waterloo, which stopped Napoleon from trying to conquer the whole of Europe.

## *The River Effra*

People walking along the Thames in Victorian times noticed a coffin floating down the river. 'How weird!' they thought, but it was eventually found to have come from West Norwood Cemetery, where the grave seemed undisturbed. People said that the grave had been dug very close to the route of the River Effra, which runs right underneath the cemetery. After a heavy rainstorm, the coffin, in the newly dug grave, had sunk into the underground river and floated right underneath the houses and gardens of south London before coming out at the Thames at Vauxhall.

## *The River Peck*

Have you ever wondered how a river starts? Often, rivers start from water that bubbles out from under the ground, and this is called a spring. The River Peck starts as a spring in a place called One Tree Hill in south London. This little spot has many stories attached to it. Among other legends it is said that Boudicca, the Queen of the ancient British tribe, the Iceni, was finally defeated here by the Romans after her army had destroyed London. They say that when she saw her army defeated, she killed herself and is buried near the Peck spring on One Tree Hill.

Queen Elizabeth I was said to have had a picnic up here under a mighty oak tree that must have been watered by the young Peck stream. She was so impressed that she knighted it, just like she would knight a hero, and it became known as 'The Honour Oak'.

Dick Turpin, the famous highwayman, would wait by the spring on the hill here, where he could spot travellers very clearly coming across Peckham Rye Common below and ride down easily on his horse, rob them and get away quickly.

These days, apart from a very short stretch of the river flowing through Peckham Rye Park, it flows underground until it enters the Thames by the Greenland Dock in Rotherhithe.

## The River Neckinger

It is thought that this river got its unusual name from the spooky things that happened at the wharf where it entered the Thames. In the 1600s, this was the place where pirates were executed. The noose on the rope that hanged them was nicknamed the 'devil's neckcloth'.

Now, a neckcloth in those days was called a 'neckinger' and so the river was named after it. A public house stood here for hundreds of years with the equally spooky name, The Dead Tree Inn.

## *The Westbourne*

Although most of this river can no longer be seen, there are two surprising places where it appears overground instead of being buried in huge pipes underground. The first is a place where Queen Caroline, King George II's wife, ordered a dam to be built across the Westbourne to make a long, winding lake called the Serpentine. This was in 1730 and she did it to make her garden, Hyde Park, more beautiful. Today, anybody can go to Hyde Park, where you can see people swimming in the lake and you can go boating or just sit by the lake and watch the swans.

The other place where the Westbourne appears above ground is, most surprisingly, in a big blue metal box-like container running right over your head on a platform of Sloane Square Underground Station. As you wait for the train, the river flows right above you and on down to the River Thames at Chelsea.

## The River Ravensbourne and Deptford Creek

The Ravensbourne has some really interesting stories of the life and history of London, beginning at a place called Caesar's Well in Kent. Every year on 1 May, a group of dancers called the Ravensbourne Morris Men dance around the well to celebrate where this river was born.

From here, the river flows eleven miles down to Deptford Bridge, where it changes its name to Deptford Creek. This is the place where so many famous events happened. The bridge over the creek was the site of the Battle of Deptford Bridge in 1497 between King Henry VII's army and peasants who were being forced to pay for a war with Scotland.

Queen Elizabeth I came to Deptford Creek, where she knighted Francis Drake for being the first Englishman to sail around the world on his famous ship, the *Golden Hinde*. She was also very pleased with him because he brought much treasure, including six tons of spices from the East Indies (worth their weight in gold in those days) and hordes of gold that he'd stolen from a Spanish galleon he'd attacked in the Pacific Ocean. It seems the Queen didn't mind a bit of piracy – if it made her rich.

# OLD FATHER THAMES

High in the hills, down in the dales
Happy and fancy free
Old Father Thames keeps rolling along
Down to the mighty sea

What does he know, what does he care?
Nothing for you or me
Old Father Thames keeps rolling along
Down to the mighty sea

He never seems to worry
Doesn't care for fortune's fame
He never seems to hurry
But he gets there just the same

Kingdoms may come, kingdoms may go
Whatever the end may be
Old Father Thames keeps rolling along
Down to the mighty sea

# 1

# THE LION KEEPER'S APPRENTICE

## December 1692

It's not true what they've said. I never stole anything. I just stole myself away along with the clothes on my back and this cursed silver collar around my neck. I would have left that behind if I could have undone it. They say I stole ten pounds in silver and one guinea. They lie. Yes, silver was stolen from the Mint, which is in the Tower, but it was not I who stole it. I am in enough trouble as it is without drawing more attention to myself by stealing or having money.

I am a poor, enslaved boy. I was born on a plantation in Barbados and became a servant in the house of my master. He left Barbados and came to London, bringing me with him.

I arrived at the Port of London on the great River Thames. Barbados is surrounded by the Caribbean Sea, but I had never been to sea. I couldn't swim. The voyage was long and the weather stormy. Great battalions of clouds followed the ship. The ship was hurled up one side of a wave and then hurtled down the other. I hoped to die then and there.

I didn't know where I was going or what was going to happen to me. I never knew my mother or father. I had no one but my master and he was not a sensible man.

After we arrived in London, he took possession of a grand house on the Strand. The Strand slopes down to the Thames. I was often sent to take messages and I would watch the barges carrying great bales of hay. Some of the men who worked on the barges had been sailors and came from Africa or the Caribbean. It cheered me to see them.

I am frightened of the sea, but I love the River Thames. I love its swift tide and the way it carries things along with it. It is free while the land is not. It flows out to the sea and moves night and day. It is full of fish, and I dream that one day I will find a small boat, wait for the outgoing tide and then let the great river take me away. Away to anywhere where I am not owned by anyone.

Anyway, word went around that a rich plantation owner had come to town and people came swarming like bees around a honeypot. My master was flattered and spent great sums of money entertaining them. The rich ladies and gentlemen drank his wine and ate his food and persuaded him

to invest what money he had in businesses that failed.

When his fortune was gone the ladies and gentlemen also left. He had to sell whatever he had. I was sold, to be an apprentice at the Tower of London. Thomas Dymock, the King's official lion tamer, was my new master.

My old master used to call me Sam, but my new master called me Leo. They thought it was a good idea to have a black boy work with the lions. They called me 'the little African boy'. I had never been to Africa, and I had never seen a lion. I was terrified. They dressed me in fancy clothes, in a cinnamon-coloured coat with a silver collar around my neck with the words, 'Thomas Dymock at the Lion Office' engraved on the collar.

The lions were as unhappy as I was. They roared and walked in circles, swishing their tails. It was dangerous to go near them. My job was to cut up their meat and feed them, to remove any unwanted bones and to clean out their den and wash it down with water from the river. It stank, and the stink and noise would make me feel sick. One keeper had been badly hurt removing old bones when a leopard had escaped and pounced upon him. Luckily, other keepers were around to help, and he recovered from his injuries. You can guess I was very, very careful. I didn't want to end up as a big cat's dinner.

The lions didn't like to be looked at, nor did any of the big cats. The leopards would urinate on you if you came too close and they would destroy anything they could claw away with their great paws. Many ladies lost their parasols, muffs and hats. I felt sympathy for the poor creatures caged up and having to put up with people staring at them. I shared their frustration, though if I had attacked any of the ladies or gentlemen who stared at me, I would have been put to death.

Yes, I was well fed, I slept in a warm bed, my clothes were of good quality – but I was not free. Mary, a woman who used to work in my master's great house in Barbados, once told a story of a wolf and a dog. It is a story I have never forgotten. I will tell it to you:

A gaunt wolf was almost dead with hunger when he happened to meet a house dog, who was passing by. 'Ah cousin,' said the dog. 'How now? Your irregular life will soon be the ruin of you. Why don't you work steadily as I do and get your food given to you regularly?'

'I would have no objection,' said the wolf, 'if I could only get a place.'

'I will easily arrange that for you,' said the dog. 'Come with me to my master and you shall share my work.'

So, the wolf and the dog went towards the town together. On the way there, the wolf noticed that the hair on a certain part of the dog's neck was very worn away, so he asked him how that had come about. 'Oh, it's nothing,' said the dog. 'That's only the place where the collar is put on at night to keep me chained up; it chafes a bit, but one soon gets used to it.'

'Is that all?' said the wolf. 'Then goodbye to you, master dog. I'd rather starve than be a well-fed slave.'

Mary, who told me the story, had been stolen from Ireland when she was just a child and brought to Barbados to work on the sugar plantation. She would have loved to run away but didn't dare. She was old and not well when we left for England and my master left her behind. I often wonder what happened to her. She was always kind to me.

I dreamt of escaping. My days were long, and my nights were interrupted by the roars coming from the lions' den and my own troubled thoughts. How to escape? It wasn't going to be easy. I was property. I had been bought and could be sold and bought again.

I used to go down to the river to fetch water to wash out the lions' den. I had two great leather buckets and went back and forth many times in a day.

Sometimes I dared the wrath of my master and took time to stand awhile and watch what was happening on the river. So many barges, wherries, ships and sails. So much to see. Many times, the river was so chock-a-block I could have stepped to the other side by jumping from one boat's deck to another. Everyone used the river to travel. There was a lot of river and not a lot of road. The roads that existed were clogged with mud and filth.

An idea was forming in my brain. If I could get aboard a barge when the tide was low, I could make my way downstream and 'disappear'. There would be no footprints, no scent for dogs to track me down. I could go in the dead of night, so no one could say they had seen me pass by. But I needed someone to be on my side. How was I to eat? Where could I stay?

That idea was growing in my head. Every time I took the buckets to the river to fetch water to sluice out the lions' enclosure, the idea took more shape. I waved to the men on the barges as they passed by. One man, in particular, I looked out for. He must have come from somewhere else, like me. Our skins were the same colour. I liked that he seemed to look out for me, too. One afternoon he pointed to the collar around my neck, and he shook his head in a sorrowful way. Would he help me get away?

It was a cold, late afternoon in December. It was already dark. The tide was low and flowing towards the sea. I left the buckets further up by the Tower and I made my way across the mud and waited for the barges to pass. They came. I waved to the man, whom I now thought of as a friend. He beckoned and I waded out to the barge without looking back. He hauled me aboard and told me to get under the canvas that covered the load on the back of the barge. I did so. I stayed, not daring to move, hoping no one had seen me clamber aboard. I knew I would be passing landmarks

that had become familiar to me: the church of All Hallows by the Tower; the docks and harbours where ships lay at anchor waiting to set off across the globe to bring back spices, tea and rice; clippers and schooners, frigates and men-o-war; whaling ships and barges with loads of coal and timber.

I waited until I was sure we had rounded the bend in the river, making towards the Royal Hospital for seamen in Greenwich that was being built at the request of Queen Mary. I looked out upon the river, the wide, glittering highway reaching to the sea, to the rest of the world! I looked astern to watch the silver and grey pleats of the river trailing the barge as it made its way downstream.

I turned around to look for'ard towards the horizon. A long, grey cloud floated just above the river. It had the shape of a river monster: a shark, an alligator. I was moving towards the unknown. But hadn't my life always been like that? I had been moved from one country to another, from one master to another, and although I'd never been beaten, nor starved,

I was owned. The collar around my neck told everyone I was not my own person but belonged to another. I thought of Barbados, of Mary, of Master Dymock, of the Tower of London. I was both there and then and here and now, floating towards tomorrow. A body in one time and place, with a head in many.

I thought, 'I'll ask my friend if I can work with him on the river. I'll stay on the river. The river is free. It doesn't stay still long enough for anyone to trap it or cage it. The people who work on the river have more freedom than those who work on the land.'

I overheard Thomas Dymock once tell this story to one of the keepers at the Tower:

The old king, King James I, was once in want of some twenty thousand pounds. He applied to the Corporation of London for the loan of that sum. The Corporation refused. The King, who thought everyone should do what he asked, was very put out and sent for the Lord Mayor and told him that they should raise the money *by hook or by crook*.

'May it please your Majesty,' said the Lord Mayor. 'We cannot lend you what we have not got.'

'You must get it,' replied the king, haughtily.

'We cannot, sire,' said the Lord Mayor.

'Then I'll compel you,' replied the king.

'But, sire, you cannot compel us,' retorted the Lord Mayor.

'No?' exclaimed King James. 'Then I'll ruin you and your city for ever. I'll remove my courts of law, my Court itself and my Parliament to Winchester or to Oxford, and make a desert of Westminster, then think what will become of you!'

'May it please your majesty,' the Mayor said, meekly but firmly. 'You are at liberty to remove yourself and your courts wherever you please. But sire, there will always be one consolation to the merchants of London: your Majesty cannot take the Thames along with you.'

Yes, I will cast my lot in with the great River Thames. I may sometimes be hungry, sometimes in danger, but whatever lies ahead, it is my life. I am my own person and this man who has helped me get free will not be the only friend I make. There are free men and women out there and I too will be free.

*A little note: This story is based on a notice that appeared in a London newssheet in December 1692 concerning 'a black boy, aged about 16, run away from Mr Thomas Dymock, at the Lyon office in the Tower. Whoever shall apprehend him shall have two Guineas reward.' Happily, nothing further is known, and we hope that, as in the story, the boy kept his freedom.*

# 2

# GRACE O'MALLEY: THE GIRL WHO BECAME A PIRATE

The River Thames had never seen anything like it! Not only was a foreign pirate ship sailing up the river, but it was going right up to the Queen's royal palace at Greenwich! The pirate in command of the ship was coming to complain (to Queen Elizabeth herself) about how she and her people were fed up with being controlled by the English! And, yes, it was a *she* – a female pirate! Who had ever heard of such a thing?

All along the river from the place where it meets the North Sea, between Kent and

Essex, and right up to the lovely royal palace on the shore at Greenwich, people were abuzz with the news. They had all heard that a pirate was coming to visit the great Queen Elizabeth I herself! They watched the ship sailing past the mud flats and salt marshes and from the riverbanks they strained to see if they could spot this terrible pirate on the deck of that ship.

But this wasn't the usual sort of pirate you hear about, with an eye patch, a big pistol, maybe a long sword and even a peg leg. No, this pirate was someone whom the Irish people called a queen – a pirate queen! She was the famous Grace O'Malley, and she was bold and courageous, and she commanded hundreds of men. They say she was braver than the men she led.

But all these men were so willing to serve her because she was the only person really fighting to keep Ireland free – free of the English who were trying to take over their lands. Because of this she was famous and was respected as a leader, not only by her own people in Ireland but also by her enemies in England.

All across the open seas from Portugal and Spain to the north coasts of Africa, the people knew and spoke of her. She had caused so much trouble for the English, who were trying to conquer the whole of Ireland.

But now she was coming to tell the Queen of England that she didn't like her land being taken over like this, and her son, whom the English had captured, should be released immediately.

Grace was a fearless pirate who had dared to sail up the Thames and had demanded to see the Queen of England. 'But why?' the people asked, and what did this wild pirate woman want Queen Elizabeth to do? They asked themselves why she wasn't afraid, because, after all, she was at war with England. And why wasn't she scared of being punished, put in prison, or even worse? After all, the punishment for piracy was death by hanging.

Well, to answer some of these questions, we have to go back to when she was just a girl, many, many years before. And back to the stories and songs that are still being told and sung by the people in the west of Ireland.

Grace O' Malley was born as the only daughter into an Irish-speaking and great seafaring family, the clan O'Malley, around 1530. Her father, Eoghan, or Owen, O'Malley, was the chieftain of the clan, but everyone called him 'Black Oak'. They were a family who controlled the land and seas of County Mayo and Galway in the west of Ireland. They traded with France and Spain and built a row of castles facing the sea to protect their territory. Anyone who fished or traded in their area would be made to pay a tax on what they took from their lands before they could pass through or anchor there. But many didn't want to pay and then the O'Malleys would attack their ships and take all that they carried, saying it was rightfully theirs since it had all come onto *their* land and into *their* waters. Sometimes, they even took the ship as well.

More than any others, the English, who were trying to control the west of Ireland, didn't want to pay tax to the Irish, as they wanted to take over the land and sea for themselves. And they wanted to make the people of Ireland pay tax to them! This just wasn't fair, and it made the O'Malley clan ruthless as pirates, terrorising any English ships that wanted to fish or trade off their coasts.

Grace was born into this family and as a child she was always headstrong and rebellious, for which she was famous all her life. She was always pestering her father to allow her to sail the seas with him. She knew that the sea was in her blood.

One day she saw her father was getting ready to go on an expedition to Spain and she suggested that she was now old enough to go with him. 'No Grace,' he said, 'seafaring is not suitable for women or girls.'

She replied, 'If I was a boy, you'd let me come with you!'

But, trying to find an excuse, he would just say things like, 'Well, your long hair isn't practical for sailing and will get caught in the ropes.' But this only had the effect of making Grace go and chop it all off, which made her father laugh at her and call her *'Granuaile'*, which means 'bald Grace'.

But Grace wasn't having any of this laughing and joking about a girl wanting to sail. She put on boy's clothes and stowed away below decks on board her father's ship. When they were well out at sea, she came up on deck and her father was amazed that she had done this. He told her to go below decks, 'It's not safe for a girl here. There's an English warship following us, and we could

be attacked. Now go down below out of harm's way!' But instead of doing that, she climbed up the rigging and looked out from the Crow's Nest on top of the mast.

This turned out to be absolutely the right thing to do, because sailors from the English ship crept up quietly and boarded her father's ship without anyone knowing. But Grace saw all of this from above. She shrieked as loudly as she could to warn her father and jumped on to the back of a sailor who was approaching him with a knife. This gave the crew enough warning to be able to fight off the English. From this moment on, Grace was known as a bit of a hero and her father had to admit she had saved his life.

Another story that people still tell of Grace is that, many years after her other three children had been born, she had her fourth child, Tibóid, who was born at sea. She was sailing back home after a long voyage of trading. She had just given birth when the ship was attacked by Algerian pirates. Hearing all the commotion coming from the deck above, she wrapped the baby in a blanket and went up on deck. In her usual way, she gave out a bloodcurdling shriek and rallied her men into action. The Algerian pirates, who were feared everywhere, were now afraid themselves. They couldn't believe their eyes that a woman was in command and was wielding a great big sword. The pirates were driven off and once more Grace saved the day.

Grace had now become the chieftainess of the O'Malley clan. She had many trading ships with an army of 200 loyal men, lands, a few stone castles and more than a thousand head of cattle, which was the real sign of an Irish chieftain's wealth.

But now, the time came when she had to fight off the English, who were taking over, bit by bit, all the land across Ireland. One by one, they managed to control many of the forty different chieftainships or clan areas in Ireland. Some they captured by force and others by promising the clan leaders they could become noble lords, earls and counts of their area, but their people would have to pay taxes to the English.

No way was Grace going to be taken over, either by force, or by letting the English make her a Countess and then, on top of that, making her people pay tax on their own land and property.

Sir Richard Bingham became the English Governor of the area of Connacht, where Grace had her lands and her castles. He was a cruel governor and preferred to use force, saying, 'The Irish will never be tamed with words but with swords' and he attacked. He took her land, killed her eldest son, Owen, stole her cattle and horses and left her people struggling to feed themselves.

But Grace still had her ships, and from this point, she became an all-out pirate and a rebel. She attacked all the English ships trying to trade with the west of Ireland. She stole the food from the ships to feed her people. Those ships couldn't follow her into the rocky bays because they were so big. Grace's galleys, being much faster and smaller, were able to sneak off through the little islands, rocks and sandbars after they'd attacked the English ships.

Bingham was furious and called her the most 'notorious woman in all the coasts of Ireland'. He tried harder to defeat her. He executed two of her stepsons and kidnapped her youngest son, Tibóid (the one who'd been born at sea during the Algerian pirates' raid) and held him as a hostage.

This was the final straw for Grace, and she knew there was only one thing to do now. First, she wrote a very polite letter to Queen Elizabeth, explaining that she only wanted to farm her land and to carry on her trading at sea, but that Sir Richard Bingham made this impossible for her and that was why she had turned to piracy. She then set sail for London.

By now, she was getting much older, already in her sixties, and this was a dangerous journey. She could have been chased and captured by other pirates sailing the seas or she could have been attacked by English ships as she sailed around southern England into the Thames and up to London.

But her risk paid off. Queen Elizabeth and her advisers were intrigued by her story and agreed to meet her.

Grace docked at the jetty outside the palace at Greenwich. How different, she thought, was this magnificent and enormous palace to her very small, bare and draughty stone castle back home in Ireland. As she walked through the long corridors with their beautiful tapestries and furnishings, she was in a completely different world from that of her hard life at sea. She thought of the hard life of her people and their little thatched cottages on the stormy west coast of Ireland.

The courtiers and ladies-in-waiting watched her and sniggered as she walked through the passageways in her very simple and rough clothes. They were used to people wearing silks and lace when they visited the Queen, but when they noticed that she walked with her head held high, they could see she was as strong as their own Queen. She had the confidence of a fearless leader.

When Grace refused to bow or curtsey to the Queen, they were quite shocked. They'd never seen a woman like this before. But Grace considered herself a Queen of her own people, just as Elizabeth was the English Queen.

Queen Elizabeth told everyone to leave her alone with the pirate. But what did they think of each other? Elizabeth was covered from head toe in rich clothes and jewels, but even though she commanded many men at sea and on land, she herself had never sailed

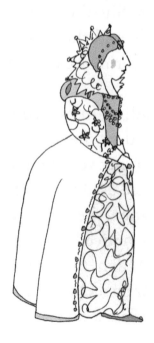

beyond the Thames. Did she envy the life of adventure that Grace had led? And Grace, as she sat with the Queen in this warm and comfortable room, did she now, as she was getting older, wish that life might have been a bit easier?

We don't know. But the story does tell us that they talked for a long time and they spoke in Latin, because Grace knew no English and Elizabeth knew no Irish. That's how we know that Grace, even though she was a pirate, had been well educated.

As two powerful women, they had much to talk about and were intrigued by each other. Grace told Elizabeth how she had been forced to become a rebel pirate because of the cruel way her people had been treated. She talked of how her son, Tibóid, was being held prisoner by Sir Richard Bingham and how they all just wanted to live in peace in their own land. Hearing this, the Queen seemed moved.

Elizabeth wrote to Bingham, ordering him to release Tibóid and allow Grace to live in peace. Grace's risky trip to London had

worked, and as her galley sailed back down the
Thames out to the open sea, perhaps Queen
Elizabeth watched it disappear, thinking just
how similar, but also how different, they were
to each other. Two very strong queens from
two completely different worlds.

# A FULL MOON

A full moon, a full tide,
a big ship anchored at the wharf's side.
Then a silent sail from the river bend,
a silver ripple marking the wend
of its quiet way towards the ship tall,
man comes alongside, no trouble at all,
stows a heavy chest, passed over the side,
then sails away on the outgoing tide.

River, river flow, river flow
River, river flow, river flow.

The tide ebbs to the estuary
where the mist comes rolling in from the sea.
A lonely shore fringed by trees,
listen close, you'll hear on the breeze

with the curlew, another call,
the boat moors, the man then hauls
the chest ashore. It changes hands.
A clink of gold, the colour of sand.

River, river flow, river flow
River, river flow, river flow.

What was in that chest? We'll never know.
It all happened so long ago.
But on quiet nights when the tide is high
and the moon is hidden by clouds in the sky,
a shadowy sail comes into view,
a voice is heard above the curlew's mew.
A clink of gold and the mists arise,
there's a cold chill down by the riverside.

River, river flow, river flow
River, river flow, river flow.

# 3

# MARY GODWIN: A CHILDHOOD BY THE RIVER FLEET

Have you heard of Frankenstein? Yes, I am sure you have, but did you know that more than two hundred and twenty years ago, Mary Shelley, who wrote *Frankenstein*, grew up in London.

Her name then was Mary Godwin and for the first four years of her life she lived with her father in a part of London called Somers Town. Sadly, her mother died not long after Mary was born, and her father was on his own with her and her big sister.

There were many French people in Somers Town. They had left France because there was a lot of fighting there. It was the time of the French Revolution. Mary heard a lot of people speaking French and she loved to try and copy what she heard.

When Mary was 4 years old, her daddy thought he needed to marry again in order to have someone help him look after the two little girls. He married a woman who already had two children, so now they were a family of four children. But Mary wasn't happy about this. She liked it being just her dad, her sister and herself.

Well, at least it was nice to go out. There were market gardens where people grew flowers and vegetables. There were fields of hay, and at harvest time it was fun to climb up onto the haystacks. Mary could see all the way to the hills of Hampstead. There were streams and ponds with ducks and geese and the goose girls would walk their flocks of geese from one field to another, so the geese could find plenty of worms and snails to eat.

Mary liked to sit on the grass by the duck pond and try to make daisy chains with the little white flowers with the golden centres that grew in their hundreds among the sweet, green grass.

The air that ruffled through the windows of their house on warm afternoons smelt of honeysuckle and new-mown hay and Mary could hear the rustle of leaves, the chirrup of birds and the clip clop of horses as they pulled the small carts of vegetables to market. There were also great kilns for making bricks and tiles.

Mary liked to watch the men working. A not so nice sight were the dust heaps: great heaps of rubbish collected from the city. Very poor people would look through the heaps, hoping to find something useful or something worth some money.

But then, a change was about to happen. The new wife decided they needed to move and open a business to make some money. Mary was ten years old when they moved to Skinner Street. Mary hated it. The house was gloomy and crumbling, and the River Fleet flowed nearby and was filthy. Mary often saw dead dogs, rats and bones floating in the river. Smithfield Market was nearby and the poor animals, taken there to be killed, would cry out. Mary would put her fingers in her ears, but nothing blocked out the sound of the creatures going to their death. The air that drifted through the open windows was foul smelling and so, more often than not, the windows stayed tightly shut.

Mary's father was now selling stationery and books for children. The books had pictures, and some were very bloodthirsty. The story of how the Cyclops ate the sailors who sailed with Odysseus was very gory indeed. Her dad taught her a poem about the River Fleet in a storm, written by a writer named Jonathan Swift:

> Sweepings from butchers' stalls, dung, guts and blood,
> Drowned puppies, stinking sprats, all drenched in mud,
> Dead cats and turnip tops came tumbling down the flood.

It seemed to Mary that this part of London was all about dirt and death. Prisoners were paraded through the streets on carts on their way to the terrible Newgate Prison. Mary longed for the quiet market gardens of Somers Town.

Now she was older she went to sit by her mother's grave in St Pancras Old Church. The only sound she heard there belonged to the River Fleet, which flowed beyond the graveyard fence. The church was very old, and the Sunday service was held there only once a month.

There were many memorials to the French people buried there who had fled the terror of the French Revolution. But it was a quiet place, where Mary could sit by her mother's grave and think her own thoughts, whereas in the crowded house at Skinner Street there was always something she was supposed to be doing.

Mary would visit her old home in Somers Town. A sandy path led her past the brickworks and kilns and the fields of hay. There were workmen's cottages and a watchmaker's shop and there was the muffin man, making his rounds with his tray of muffins in front of him. It was good to hear snatches of French being spoken. Mary would wave and say, 'Bonjour Madame, Bonjour Monsieur.'

But there were other people living in their old house now, so Mary would have to return to the gloomy house on Skinner Street. Mary began to make up stories. Many of them were gloomy.

One night there was a tremendous storm. Mary opened her little window in the tiny room she shared with her sister at the top of the house. Lightning forked through the sky and lit up the torrent of the River Fleet below. The current was so strong that bones and carcasses of dead animals were hurled up into the air and landed again with a splash and were swept away. It was as if the lightning, the storm and the power of the water were giving life back to those dead bones.

Mary got up, lit a candle and found a book of ancient Greek myths. She read the story of how the giant Prometheus created human beings. He came of the race of the Titans, a giant people who were born on the earth before humankind. Prometheus saw that humankind must be made from the earth, since only gods could be made of a heavenly substance. He took handfuls of earth and kneaded them with water into the shape of a god. What separated people from all other animals was that, while animals crept on their bellies, or ran and trotted about on all fours, people walked upright on two feet. While other creatures looked down towards the earth from which they came, humans looked up towards the heavens.

Mary looked up from the book she was reading and out of the window. The lightning and thunder continued and the River Fleet seemed to bubble and boil. Mary could easily believe that some of those bones that were being swept away in the fast-flowing flood might take on a life of their own.

She continued to read the ancient story. Prometheus had a brother, Epimetheus, and his task was to provide the creatures of the earth with what they needed to survive. He gave swiftness to the tiger, strength to the lion, wings to the birds and fins to the fishes; the fox was given cunning, the wolf ferocity and the elephant its huge size and its thick, leathery skin.

But what was to be given to humans? They could never have claws like those of the tiger, nor speed like that of the horse; humans couldn't fly like an eagle or grow horns like a deer. Even the little hare was faster and the spotted leopard better at hiding among the trees. How could humans live in a world full of creatures such as these? Human skin was fine and soft, human teeth and nails were small.

The truth was that Epimetheus had used up all the gifts in his possession and had nothing special left to give to humans, so he went to his brother Prometheus and asked him to help. 'We must give them something from heaven,' answered Prometheus. 'Something beyond the power of all others on earth.'

So, Prometheus went up to heaven and stole fire from the sun. Now humans had the heavenly gift of fire. Fire could warm, scare away dangerous beasts, and cook food. Fire could melt down metals to make tools to dig and plant the earth, grow crops, make images and statues, coins and ornaments. Fire helped people become strong and powerful beyond the strength of their own bodies.

Mary read late into the night and when she finally went back to her bed to sleep, she had strange dreams of a man made of earth and fire and water, a man who came to life and was very powerful …

*A little note*: *When Mary grew up and became a writer and wrote her famous book* Frankenstein *in 1818, she gave it the subtitle,* The Modern Prometheus.

# 4

# FROST FAIRS ON THE FROZEN RIVER THAMES

Susanna was really excited because she and her two older sisters, Elizabeth and Mary, were going with their father, John Evelyn, from Deptford to London Bridge where the famous Frost Fair was happening. Everybody had been talking about it. It was going to be so much fun! Just like a carnival on the ice, they said!

They travelled by coach, because their normal route, by river on one of the Thames wherries, was impossible as the river was frozen over. On the way, they saw things that were terrible. They could see many people begging. Many were hungry, as not much food could be brought into London in these difficult times and only the people with money could afford to pay for good food. But the children knew their father always tried to help the poor. It was lucky he was important and quite wealthy because he could work on improving the streets and buildings of London and was always looking into the affairs of charities, making sure that ordinary Londoners were not forgotten.

As they approached London Bridge, the excitement grew. They could hear laughing, music playing and the general hubbub of lots of people having fun. As they walked down the steps towards what was normally a place where boats were coming and going, where ferries were crossing the river and where people would be fishing, they now saw that everything had changed.

The whole of the river was completely frozen solid – a white mass of ice where before there had been flowing water. There was a whole street on the ice made up of tents, booths and stalls that people had set up like a street market. They saw crowds of people playing football, nine-pin bowling and ice skating. There were puppet shows and sleigh rides across the ice and you could even have your name printed on a beautiful souvenir card, as a whole heavy printing press had been set up on the ice.

The watermen, who couldn't earn their fares by ferrying people across the Thames, were setting up stalls where they sold little toys made of tin or wood. They sold coffee, beer and brandy to the adults and hot chocolate to the children. There were butchers, bakers and barbers here, too, because they got more trade now than if they had stayed in their shops

in town. Everywhere you looked, people were eating, drinking and having so much fun in this winter wonderland.

Susanna, Mary and Elizabeth walked among all this exciting and wonderful activity. They were thrilled to see everything just like a carnival. Elizabeth was quiet, but kept sneezing as it really was bitterly cold,

which made her father look at her with a lot of concern. All of their brothers, apart from John, had died as young children and so father was always concerned about their health, and now he was worrying about her sneezing.

He directed them to one of the great big fires where they were roasting a whole ox for people who were hungry from all their activity on the ice. He thought she could warm up standing by it and maybe have something warm to eat. They looked at the fire, which was burning on the ice, but it seemed to be having no effect in melting it. It was said that the ice was so thick it went down solid for twenty feet and stretched for many miles on either side of London Bridge.

All this time Mary was talking about everything that interested her, especially what people were wearing. 'Oh, look at that bonnet!' and 'Look at that beautiful shawl! How stylish. How elegant.' 'Look at the lace, that cashmere, those shoes!' 'Oh, dear, look at that woman! How vain! How showy!'

Just then, she spotted something that made her stop in her tracks. 'Oh, look there,' she said. 'That's sable. They've got sable here!'

'What's sable?' asked Susanna.

'It's only the most beautiful and expensive fur you can find, that's what it is!' Mary said, as Elizabeth sneezed again. 'It's as light as a feather, sparkling and so incredibly beautiful.'

They looked over and saw some rather wealthy-looking men, wearing big collars of sable and fur hats made of exactly the same thing. The sable really was beautiful. It seemed to shimmer, and the colour was somewhere between beige, brown and gold, with an occasional touch of silver and black. 'It's called soft gold,' said Mary, 'because it's as valuable, if not more valuable than gold itself.'

She heard the people saying that these men were from Muscovy or Russia and they had just arrived in England by boat when the freeze started. Their ship had got locked in the ice further downriver. So, every day they brought their cargo of furs,

by horse-drawn sleigh, upriver to the frost
fair. Wealthy Londoners were delighted
with this most exquisite fur and paid lots of
money to have some. It was just the right
time because everyone wanted something to
keep themselves warm.

Their father went straight over to see if
he could buy a warm hood for Elizabeth.
It certainly was expensive, but the moment
she put it on she stopped sneezing.

Just then, Susanna noticed a little crowd
gathering to one side of these fur traders,
listening to a story told by the Muscovites
in their thick Russian accents. There was a
young boy there, with very high cheek bones
and almond-shaped blue eyes, maybe the son
of one of the traders, as he looked very similar
and he was able to tell the story they were
telling in English. It was the famous Russian
tale of *Morozko*, or 'Father Frost'.

Susanna loved listening to stories, and
she sat down with her father and sisters to
listen to these strange people telling the story.
This was more exciting than she could say,

and she and her family listened awestruck to what she thought was an extraordinary story:

Many years ago, in a very distant land, there was a man and his wife. They had both been married before, but their former partners had died and so they had married again. Each of them had a daughter from their earlier marriage. Manya, the daughter of the woman, was mean and spiteful, while Annika, the daughter of the man, was loving and kind. The woman loved only her daughter and left Annika to work all day long, doing all the hard housework. The poor girl had to clean the house all on her own and her stepmother often gave her a mighty wallop. Each day, the woman grew to hate the man's daughter more and more.

One day, in the middle of a cold, hard winter, the stepmother decided that Annika should be taken into the forest and left to fend for herself. Of course, her father didn't want that to happen, but his wife was so horrible, bossy and nasty that he was scared of her.

Sadly, he loaded his sleigh with all sorts of foods and warm blankets for Annika so that she might be able to stay warm and fed until she found somewhere to go or someone to help her. But his wife got her daughter, Manya, to secretly take everything off the sleigh while she distracted her husband by telling him which direction to go in.

Deep in the forest, her father left Annika sitting all alone under a tree. But then after a very short while she heard the rustling and cracking of branches and a voice spoke to her, 'Are you warm my dear child?'

'That's a strange question', she thought. 'It's freezing!' Then she remembered the stories of Morozko, or Father Frost and she knew this could only be him. She'd heard that he rewarded people who were kind and polite but punished people who were rude and nasty, so she decided not to complain about the cold. 'Yes, Father Frost, I'm warm.'

He asked her several times and came closer and closer, and it got colder and colder. But each time, she answered that she was warm, even though her eyelashes had turned white with frost.

'You're a good girl,' he said to her and he wrapped her in the softest and most beautiful blanket, which kept her warm all night and when she woke up, she was wearing a beautiful bonnet and a collar of sable.

At her feet were gifts of food, shawls and quilts and a chest filled with sparkling jewels.

In the meantime, her father was now feeling so bad that he came back to the forest to rescue Annika. When he got there, he was overjoyed to see that not only was she still alive but she was snug and warm and was surrounded by precious gifts. They put them all onto the sleigh and went back home.

When the stepmother saw all the riches that Father Frost had given Annika, she immediately said that her own daughter should be taken to the forest to spend a night there. But this time, she made sure that Manya had plenty of warm clothes and tons of food to eat. Of course, she was hoping she'd also come back with wonderful riches.

So, the man took his wife's daughter into the forest and left her sitting under the same tree, covered in so many blankets, eating all the cheese, pies and roast chicken her mother had given her. Then, after a very short while, she too heard the rustling and cracking of branches and when Father Frost asked her, 'Are you warm my dear child?' she said, 'Of course I'm not, you stupid old man! Can't you see I'm shivering? Anyway, it's too cold to waste time. Where are my presents and my box of jewels?'

'Oh, don't worry, my dear, I'll give you what you deserve! And I'll give you a sleigh to go home right now. You don't have to stay all night in the forest. People freeze to death, you know.'

And straight away, a sleigh appeared loaded with boxes. 'Now go straight home, dear, and make sure *not* to peep into the boxes before you get home.'

Manya was delighted to have so many boxes and, yippee!, she didn't have to spend all night in that horrible forest like stupid Annika. The sleigh started suddenly speeding across the snow and in no time, it was back in her village. But as she got down off the sleigh in front of the house, all the neighbours were laughing at her and she saw that, instead of horses pulling the sleigh, there were three fat pigs grunting at her.

Her mother came out of the house in a flash and immediately started to pull the boxes down and she and Manya started to open them, one after another. But what did they find? In the first was a whole mob of crows croaking loudly and flying and flapping right at them. In the next were only pebbles, in the next was mud and each box was worse than the last.

In the meantime, Annika's father took her by the hand and rode away to a new home and a happy new life, leaving the wicked wife and her mean daughter forever.

As Susanna walked away, she had a big smile on her face from hearing such an exotic story from Russia. Elizabeth felt as lucky as Annika because, in her warm bonnet, her sneezing had stopped completely. Mary's mind was buzzing with everything she had seen. Later, she would write about all the fashions and styles from that wonderful day, in the funny book, *The Ladies Dressing Room Unlocked*, which gently poked fun at it all.

***A little note***: *We know all this because their father, John Evelyn, wrote in his diaries and in his books about the Frost Fairs and about many other interesting things that happened on the River Thames and in London more than three hundred years ago.*

# 5

# A NEAR ESCAPE

Dear children, I am an old lady now and I live in Barking in Essex but when I was a little girl, I used to live in Canning Town near the Royal Victoria Dock, which is on the River Thames. My dad came from Nigeria. He was a sailor and worked on the huge ships that went between the Caribbean and West Africa. There were many sailors from West Africa, the Caribbean, India and China in Canning Town in those days.

My mum worked as well and had all kinds of jobs: in a factory that made margarine, in another that made jam and sweets. That was the best because she got to bring home sweets. We didn't see my dad as much as we wanted, as he was away at sea.

Then one day, we were told he would never come back. He had been swept off the deck of a ship by an enormous wave.

My dad used to go to a sailors' club in Canning Town. Some of his friends came to visit us after dad died and gave us some money that they had collected. Then my mum got a job at an enormous factory called Tate & Lyle's Sugar Refinery. She worked long hours and when she got home, she was very tired, so I used to make the supper and mum would go to bed the same time as I did.

It was in the middle of the night on the 1st of February 1953 when I woke up and heard the noise of the wind. I could hear the clattering of the roofs on the neighbour's sheds, the slamming of gates on their hinges and the rattling of loose doors and outhouses.

I woke up and looked out of the window. The river was outside our house. We lived in an upstairs flat and the water was halfway up the side of the downstairs flat. I woke mum. Mum screamed, 'Oh no, Mrs Waller is down there with her children. They'll drown!'

Mum was a quick thinker. She stripped the sheets from our beds and tied them together to make a rope. She then tied one end to the bedpost and opened our window. Then tied the other end on to me and said, 'I'll lower you down to their window. Bang on it, tell them to open it and we'll get them up here.'

I was frightened, but I knew mum wouldn't let me fall, so that's what I did. Mrs Waller and her three children were standing on their kitchen table. She managed to open the window and helped little Elsie out for me to carry. She was four years old. She wound her legs and arms around me, and mum tugged on the rope of sheets, and I clambered up using my arms and legs with the wind howling around us. I passed Elsie through the window to mum.

Down again I went and did the same with Bertie, who was six years old. Mrs Waller had a baby. Mum shouted down to her, 'Strap the baby to you. Tie the sheet tight and then come up!'

Mrs Waller was not like mum. She was terrified that she would fall and she was frightened of the wind and the ever-rising water. There were heavy, empty casks that had been washed away from the docks and they were banging against the walls of the house.

Mum shouted down again, 'Come on, Mrs Waller, or you and your baby will drown, then what will little Elsie and Bertie do?'

Mrs Waller clambered out and clung to the rope of sheets. Mum and I tugged and pulled and soon Mrs Waller appeared above the windowsill. We helped her in, unstrapped the baby and mum gave them all some soup that was still warm from supper. The electricity and gas weren't working, so that's all we could give them, but we wrapped the children in whatever blankets we had. Mrs Waller wrapped the baby in an eiderdown, and she stared from one to the other of her children as if she couldn't believe they had survived.

Above the howling of the wind, we could hear the bells of police patrol cars and police whistles. We huddled together until morning came and then there was a call from below. We looked out and there were two men in a rowing boat. They had come to rescue us. The rowing boat had a name, it was called the *Mayflower*.

It took ages to get us all in, using ropes and a ladder that the men had brought with them, then they rowed us away from our house down the street that was now a river. There were others in rubber dinghies and rowing boats, borrowed from the boating pools at Poplar and Barking Parks. Horses and carts splashed through the water. Army lorries were taking people from their waterlogged houses.

We were taken to St Margaret's Convent, where the nuns had set up a rescue centre. When we got there, Bertie couldn't stop chattering. He was telling anybody who would listen about how he had watched the river rise, how it had swept away sheds and handcarts, how it had chased the police cars and how he had watched a dog trying to swim to dry land. Other people told how the flood waters had swept into the streets. It slapped against doors and windows, burst them open and tugged things from shelves and cupboards and swept them out into the streets. The Salvation Army had come out in rubber dinghies and passed hot tea from thermos flasks and biscuits up to people trapped in upstairs rooms.

I was much older than many of the children and the nuns were busy trying to get everyone warm and dry and something to eat, so I said to one of the nuns, 'I'll tell the little ones a story to settle them down.' My dad had been a good storyteller, so I told them a story that he'd told me. This is the story of how the sun, the moon and the star children came to be in the sky:

It was a long time ago when Sun, Moon and the star children all lived together on earth. There were mountains and valleys, there were forests and fields, there were oceans, rivers, lakes, waterfalls and deep underground waters that would spring up from the earth.

Sun, Moon and the star children lived in a small house on the top of a small hill. Sun loved the water. Sun loved to look at his own bright, shiny reflection in the water.

He liked to make water sparkle. He loved the sound of it trickling and gurgling and splishing and splashing. So, every day he went out to spend time with water.

One day, Water said to Sun, 'How come you never invite me to visit you? If we're friends, I should be able to come to where you live.'

'Oh,' said Sun, 'I am afraid that's not possible because Moon and I and the star children have only a very small place and I don't think there would be room for you.'

Water didn't like this answer and said, 'Well, if you won't invite me to your place then I won't be your friend anymore.' Water then disappeared deep underground.

Sun was very upset. He stayed for a long while, hoping Water would reappear, but Water didn't, and Sun went back and was very miserable. He was miserable for more than a day, more than a night, more than a week. Moon was fed up with him and said, 'Go and invite Water to come here if it'll cheer you up.'

Sun immediately went to where he last saw Water and called out, 'Moon says you can come and visit. I'll go back and wait for you and get things ready to welcome you.'

Water immediately bubbled back up to the surface and made arrangements to visit Sun, Moon and the star children. Water was so excited he went around inviting all the waters: the rivers, the streams, the pools, the lakes, the puddles, the waterfalls, the underground springs and even the ocean. And with the ocean came all the creatures who live there: the whales, the dolphins, the sharks, the seahorses, the starfish, the octopus, the flatfish, the fat fish, the eels, the stingrays, the crabs, the lobsters, the shrimps and so many others.

Meanwhile, Sun, Moon and the star children were getting ready for Water's visit. Moon then heard a deep rumbling sound coming from a long way off.

She looked out of the door and called Sun to come and look. Water was on its way. Water was now a giant wave that came rushing over the forests and fields, cascading down the hillsides towards their own little house.

'Go back, go back!' they both shouted. But Water didn't go back.

Quickly they gathered the star children together and brought them outside. Then they held hands and together they jumped up and up and up and up into the sky, while down below Water covered their little house.

They were tired and rested on a bank of cloud. Sun was fast asleep when Moon and the star children tip-toed to the other side of the world. When Sun woke up, he stretched and set out to look for Moon and the star children. He travelled around the Earth and when he was one side of the Earth, that was daytime and the earth was warmed by the sun. Where he was not, it was night and Moon shone down with a silvery light and the star children twinkled in the dark.

I will never forget that night. When the water went down, we went back home and helped Mrs Waller clean up her flat. There was rubbish and filth from the streets mixed up with her own things. Any food she had in her cupboards had to be thrown out. Everyone in the street helped each other and we were helped with money from the Lord Mayor's Distress Fund. Mrs Waller was able to buy some new furniture, as all her old furniture was destroyed.

After a while, everything was back to normal, except I still dream of floods. If I have had a very vivid dream, I get up and look out of the window to make sure it hasn't happened again.

Bertie never stopped talking about that dreadful night. When he grew up, he became a policeman, so he could be ready to help people if there was another disaster.

*A little note: Amazingly, no one in Canning Town drowned that night, but others did – many in Essex and across the sea in the Netherlands. It was a storm surge driven by a hurricane that crashed against the east coast. The waters of the North Sea were whipped up to massive tidal levels, which smashed through sea-wall defences. Since then, the Thames Barrier has been built across the river at Woolwich to protect London.*

# DARK RIVER

Water finds a way, nothing stops it.
Raindrops make small rivulets, meet
tributaries,
drops join, mingle, unite, flow,
nothing stops water.
Raindrops swell the rivers.

Water always finds a way.
It seeps, trickles, dribbles, drops,
slow, silent, constant and
when the time is right, it takes its chance:
surges, gushes, explodes,
sweeps all before it.

This River Thames, deceptively tame,
biddable even, banked and barriered,
allowing boats to run to timetables –
this river joined forces
with the North Sea in 1953,
swamped the low-lying land.

It came at night, leapt over sea
walls
constructed to keep people 'safe',
ravaged islands and coasts
like any Viking invader, destroying,
killing.

Keep this in mind: water always finds a way.
The Celts called it 'Dark River'
and gave it human sacrifice.
River Thames, you are a dark river:
it is not *if* you will rise
but *when*.

# 6

# SAFE AT LAST: REFUGEES ON THE WANDLE

The Le Bon family didn't know what to do. The King of France had made a new law that said Huguenots, like *they* were, were no longer welcome in France, which was *their* home as much as anyone else's. Although Huguenots were Christian and French, just like the King was, they had their own way of being Christian and the King didn't like them for this and wanted to punish them.

It was dangerous for them to stay in France. Many of their friends had been put in prison, some had had their children taken away from them and they'd even heard of people being killed because of this new law. And now people were telling them they weren't allowed to leave the country. They felt they had no other choice but to try to leave France, even though it was illegal to do so.

But what could they do? They knew their mother was too ill to travel to the coast to get on a ship for England. They couldn't just leave her. But their father insisted that the two big brothers, Jean-Paul and Antoine, who were now almost completely grown up and working in the weaving trade, and their little sister, Lysbeth, who was not quite eleven yet, should travel that very night to the coast and get on a ship for England. This was probably safer because, under cover of darkness, they had more chance of not being stopped and sent back. Papa and their mother (or 'Maman' in French) would join them later when she was better.

Maman called them over and gave each of them a little bundle with just a few warm clothes, some bread, a little of her homemade cheese and a small bag of gold coins to pay for the journey. They were surprised that she had this all arranged and that they had to leave so soon. She and Papa must have been planning it for some time. Lysbeth clung to her *Maman*, not wanting to leave her when she was ill, but her lovely brother whispered

that it wouldn't be long before they'd all be together, safe and sound in England, when *Maman* was better. But now it really was time that they must leave.

They had to walk to the sea, but since they lived quite close to the coast, it only took them a couple of hours. When they got to the little harbour, they were surprised to see an old friend of the family who led them over to a small fishing boat where the skipper was waiting for them. A little family, with two frightened-looking children, were already on board. Before they knew what was happening, their friend helped them on board, the boat pushed off and their friend was waving them goodbye from the shore. Lysbeth was completely exhausted and fell into a deep sleep with the gentle rocking of the waves.

When she woke up, she saw huge white cliffs and the skipper said he must leave them on the beach here and they would get an English boat to take them to London. Now was the time to share their bread and cheese with the other family, who looked so relieved to have escaped from France. The frightened little children were now laughing, skipping and splashing in the waves.

Eventually, they boarded a big barge with red sails. As they travelled on past the famous White Cliffs of Dover and into the Thames, the father of the other family got chatting with Jean-Paul and Antoine. When he found out they were weavers, he said he'd heard that French weavers, dyers and hatmakers were being welcomed on a river called the Wandle. 'You see, the English have seen how well the French silk weavers work in other parts of London. Everyone knows that we make some of the finest silk, linen and felt cloth that you can buy and people in England are keen to buy what we make.'

By the time they docked in London, Jean-Paul and Antoine had learned a lot about this little river that flowed into the Thames and had decided they'd take Lysbeth to the banks of the Wandle to see if they could start a new life there together.

And at this point, let's just leave them there, so we can find out more about those river banks that they had never heard of before, but which seemed to have a lot to offer them. We'll return to them in a little while to find out how their story ends.

Of all the many rivers of London that flow into the Thames, there's one that, even though it's not very long, has probably been one of the most heavily worked rivers in the world. Because of this, the Wandle has many stories to tell. It's only about nine miles long but for hundreds of years people were using its very fast-flowing waters to help them to grind their corn, provide them with delicious fish and healthy watercress and clean and soften their sheep wool to spin it into yarn and weave it into cloth.

We know that the Romans and the Anglo-Saxons used big water wheels, which turned as the river flowed. These drove big millstones that helped them to grind the corn much finer and quicker and this made the bread smoother than the rough, gritty loaves the ancient Britons would have known, and which often cracked their teeth.

By the 1500s and 1600s, people were moving to the banks of the Wandle from other parts of London because, using the power of this wonderful little river, it meant they could earn more money than in other places. They built many waterwheels so that, in a very short time, the Wandle was the place

where many products were made. Here, as well as corn and flour mills, you would find mills for softening leather for shoes, bags and belts, mills for paper, cotton cloth called calico, dyes for colouring the cloth, malt for making beer and mills for copper, iron, oil and even gunpowder! All of these were manufactured using up to sixty or seventy water mills, powered by this special little river that flowed so fast down to the Thames.

By the time of Queen Victoria, the Wandle was a place where some famous people had set up workshops that helped young apprentices to learn very special trades. William Morris and his friend William de Morgan came to the River Wandle when they found the water there was ideal for making dyes.

William Morris was concerned that so many goods were now being made in dark, dangerous and crowded factories where the children and young people employed there worked for long, long hours with little air and not enough light. On the Wandle, his apprentices could learn the traditional trades of dyeing with dyes made from the ground – bark of trees, onions, flowers and plants. They would be taught to weave, make tapestries and carpets and even the beautiful stained glass that you often see in churches and important buildings.

The apprentices had bright and airy workshops and, as they worked, they heard the sounds of the river and the birds and looked out onto green meadows and woods. After work, they would get good food and a comfortable bed to sleep in. It might have been this that helped them to make such beautiful and special things that made people want to pay extra to get these lovely products. This was so different to all the child workers in other parts of London, who didn't have such good working conditions, or such thoughtful employers.

A couple of hundred years before these Victorians came to this very special river, there was another group of people who made big changes here. They were refugees and they had been forced to leave their homes in

France because of their religion. They were the Huguenots, and here we pick up the story of that one family whom we have met before, Jean-Paul, Antoine and Lysbeth Le Bon.

Once the little Le Bon family arrived at the River Wandle, they settled in quickly. Maybe this was because there were other Huguenots living there already. Hearing their own language being spoken, it made them feel a little bit at home, even though they were in a strange land where everyone else spoke English. Of course, they couldn't speak that language yet, but the English people seemed to be very welcoming to them.

They soon learned this was because they thought Huguenots were very good at their work. They liked their fine weaving, the beautiful ribbons and flannel cloth and felt hats they were so good at making. Now everyone was talking about how they had a way of making a red dye called 'Wandsworth Scarlet' that didn't run and drip away in the rain, like other red dyes did before. It was soon being used for soldiers' uniforms and for the special red hats that the important priests, the cardinals, all over Europe wanted to wear – so that if they went out in the rain, they wouldn't have red dye running down their faces.

Because Huguenots were so respected in England for their special skills, Lysbeth and her two big brothers felt more and more at home each day. Antoine soon found work weaving fine cotton with another refugee friend from France and it didn't take long for people to find out that Jean-Paul knew about making dyes to colour silk and cotton fabric. He started working at one of the watermills that rumbled and creaked as the water turned the wheel, as it ground and pounded the colour into dye. And Lysbeth was helping the calico girls, who had to lay out the cotton calico cloth in the fields, where the rain and the sun would bleach it until it was nice and white, ready to be printed with colourful patterns.

Soon, three years had passed, and even though they were happy with their new lives, there was always a sadness too. They hadn't heard from their mother and father, who were still in France, but they still hoped they were safe. When he'd finished his work at the weaving and shared a meal with his brother

and little sister, Antoine would walk along the river to the new French chapel in the village of Wandsworth, where the Wandle joins the Thames. There he would pray.

He prayed a lot. First of all, he prayed for the safety of his mother and father. He prayed for all his friends, too, who were still in France. Whenever he had free time, he was in the chapel praying. He always thought of the people who were suffering or homeless and he prayed for poor people who didn't have enough to eat.

He and Jean-Paul and Lysbeth had been so lucky to have escaped all those horrible things that were happening to people in France. They'd found safety and been welcomed in England. But he knew of all the suffering back home in France, and this made him sad.

Well, it happened that a terrible storm came whipping up the Thames and along the valley of the Wandle. The wind howled. There were loud claps of thunder and great flashes of lightning. The rain pelted down, and everyone took shelter at home. They could hear the clattering and banging of the shutters against the windows. Anything that wasn't tied down was blown into the air.

'Oh, please don't go out in the storm tonight, Antoine,' said Lysbeth. 'It's such a terrible storm like we've never known before.'

'You're right, my precious,' Antoine answered. 'I don't need to go to the chapel in such wild weather. I can say my prayers at home tonight in our own little safe house. The good Lord will understand.'

Everyone settled down for the night and Antoine pulled his warm flannel cloak over himself as he lay down on his bed. Outside, the wind was roaring and thunder seemed to shake the house. Antoine's cloak seemed to mysteriously fall away from him, as if someone were pulling it off his bed. The wind had blown all the candles out in the house much earlier, so he lit another to see where the cloak was on the floor.

Once again, he pulled that warm cloak over him and tried to sleep again. Once more, it seemed as if someone was pulling the cloak off the bed. Jean-Paul and Lysbeth were in their beds asleep, but whatever Antoine did to try and keep his warm flannel cloak on his bed, again and again it just wouldn't stay there. 'Well,' thought Antoine, 'I can't sleep, and I can't keep myself covered up, I might as well go to chapel and pray.'

He wrapped himself in the flannel cloak and walked along by the river through the howling wind and pelting rain to the chapel. He prayed for his mother and he prayed for his father. He prayed for his friends still in France. He prayed for those who didn't have enough to eat and for the homeless and the suffering people. When he eventually got back home, he said to Jean-Paul, who let him in, 'Well, of all the nights we could pray, this is the night when our prayers really are needed!'

As he entered the house, the lightning flashed and the thunder roared. The wind blasted behind him, crashing and banging the shutters and the rain burst its way into the house before they had time to shut the door against it.

'Now give me your cloak, Antoine,' said his brother, 'and I'll dry it by the fire!'

As Jean-Paul helped him to take it off, he stepped back in amazement. Hardly able to speak clearly, he whispered, 'Feel it, Antoine, feel it! It's completely dry. You've come through the worst storm I've ever known and there's not a drop of water on your cloak!'

Antoine remained very quiet, sensing this was true. He whispered something about a miracle. As they got into bed, the brothers felt so calm they didn't even notice how everything had become quiet and the storm seemed to have stopped as quickly as it had started.

Next morning, they were all up early, and instead of feeling tired after a long night, each one felt strangely well rested as if they'd slept for many hours. There was a gentle tap on the door. They all got up to go and answer it, but her two brothers stepped back to let Lysbeth open the door. Standing outside were Maman and Papa.

Was that a miracle? Who knows? What do you think?

# SPRING TO STREAM: WHAT'S IN A NAME?

There are so many names for little rivers.
Here are some put into a poem:

Spring, stream, beck and burn
Little rivers in their turn
Starting small they slowly grow
Getting bigger as they flow

All these names are little becks
The Fleet, the Wandle and the Peck
Many names for brook and burn
A rill's a little stream, I learn

Down the hills and 'cross the land
At last, they come to Thames's strand
Down, down to the sea
Here's a list for you and me:

Rill, runnel, rivulet
brook, bourn, burn and beck
rindle, creek and then outlet
tributary and brooklet
channel, ditch and on we go
All are part of Thames's flow

# 7

# THE SILVER DARLINGS

My name is Ellen and I am fourteen years old. I live in Wapping, and I go to work every day with my friend, Peggy. Both of us work in the spice mill in Cinnamon Street. The year is 1931.

We package and label the spice boxes. The spices come in big ships from all over the world and are unloaded off the ships at the docks in Wapping. The smell of the spices is the first thing you smell when you get out of the station at Wapping – cloves, nutmeg and cinnamon.

Peggy's dad is a tugboat man, and it is an amazing sight to see the little tugs get those big ships into the docks. The dockers unload the big crates of spices and store them in the warehouses and from there they come to the spice mill where I work.

Inside, the mill is noisy and dusty and some of the girls do get a nasty cough from the dust. But we do enjoy working together. We all come from big families and sometimes it's good to get away from looking after the little ones. Our mums take turns working the early shifts, cleaning the Great Eastern Railway offices in Tooley Street. That's across the river, which means our mums have to get up when it's still dark and walk along the river and cross over at Tower Bridge to get to their work on time.

One morning, Peggy was coughing so badly she wasn't able to come to work with me. I was really upset for her. When I got home late afternoon, I went round to their flat. It was above *our* flat, in the tenement block where we lived in Old Gravel Lane.

Mrs Duggan was home and she was really worried about Peggy. She had boiled a kettle on the fire and Peggy was sitting over a basin of steaming hot water with some liniment in it and a towel over her head. The steam was meant to help her to breathe. Peggy came out from under the towel with her face all red and sweating but she was still struggling to breathe. 'You need a doctor, Mrs Duggan,' I said. 'Peggy needs to see a doctor.'

'I can't afford the doctor, Ellen. Mr Duggan had an accident the other day when getting one of the big ships into the docks. His tug was rammed at the back and he nearly drowned. He's recovering but he's not able to work. I can't work either, as I must be here to look after them both.'

Just then, all Peggy's little sisters and brothers came in from playing outside. There were six of them. The room was now really crowded and then Mrs McMahon came to the door with a big pot of rabbit stew she had made for the family. Mrs McMahon said, 'Come on Mary' (that was Mrs Duggan's name), 'share this out among the children and make sure you eat as well. You have to keep up your strength with all this trouble that's come upon you.'

I left to go and help my mum with the tea and the little ones, but all the time I was worrying about Peggy.

Just then, mum said, 'I've just heard that Frankie Sullivan has tripped when going down Old Wapping Stairs and twisted his ankle. He's sitting on the steps with his barrow of herring to sell and not able to walk. There'll be a lot of people here who won't have anything for their tea tonight.'

I said, 'Mum, I'll go and help him, as long as he shares the money with me, then I can help pay for a doctor for Peggy.'

Before mum could say a word, I was out the door and racing down towards Old Wapping Stairs. The steps are very slippery and lead down to the river.

Frankie was the same age as me and we'd been friends since we were little. 'Let me take the barrow, Frankie, and I'll sell all I can – but would it be alright if we go half and half with the money?' I told him I wanted to help Mrs Duggan pay for a doctor for Peggy.

Well, Frankie knew Peggy as well. We'd all grown up together: in and out of each other's flats, eating around each other's kitchen tables. I took the barrow of herring and set off for the tenements. Herring were popular. They were good for you and they were cheap. You could get six for a penny. They were the 'silver darlings', called that because of their glistening silver bellies and because, without them, many of us would have been very hungry. The gulls loved them too, so I had to watch for them swooping down towards the barrow. There's an old saying, 'Of all the fish that swim in the sea, the herring is the King.'

Around the tenements I went, calling out, 'Herring, fresh herring, six for a penny!' I walked around all the streets and alleys that led off of Old Gravel Lane until the barrow was empty. I was hoarse from crying out, so my voice now had a funny whistling sound. But I sold them all. The 'silver darlings' had saved the day.

I had twelve copper pennies jingling in my pocket and I knew that there was a good, kind doctor called Doctor Salter who, with five other doctors, had a surgery on Jamaica Road. They'd come out to poor families for sixpence. I knew this for a fact, as I had a friend who lived in Bermondsey, and she told me how kind those doctors were when her dad was really ill.

I ran to the Sullivans' house where Frankie was now sitting with his leg stretched out in front of him, with his poor swollen ankle all bandaged up. I gave him six of the pennies and then ran to the river, back to Old Wapping Stairs. Frankie had an older brother, John, and he had a rowing boat. Luckily, he was there, and once I explained what I wanted to do, he rowed me across the river.

I ran to the surgery on Jamaica Road. Dr Salter was there. He asked me questions about Peggy and then called for one of the nurses who worked there and gave her instructions, medicine and money for the ferryman and told us to hurry along. He wouldn't take the sixpence I offered him, but he told me he'd pay for the nurse. As I said, he was a good man and cared about us poor people. We were back across the river in no time and then to Peggy's flat.

The nurse had brought tubes and pumps and vapour rubs for Peggy's chest and when she came out, she said, 'Your friend will be alright but I don't think she can continue working at the Spice Mill.'

'Maybe,' I said, 'she can sell herring like I did today' and I told her the story of how that came about. The nurse said there was a story about the herring and she told it to me and now I am telling it to you:

Once upon a time, the fish decided they wanted to compete to see which were the best and most beautiful fish. The sun would be the judge. It was decided that all the fish should gather just as the sun rose above the horizon, so, when the first light appeared, the fish began to make their way to the meeting point.

The herring got there first as the herring swim near the surface of the sea and swim very fast. They were a fine sight, silver, slick and bright as mercury and so many of them. The shark, big and cruel in his grey coat, came swimming up from below but he was confused by the silvery light from the fish above him and he lost his way.

The cuttlefish took such a long time putting on her nicest face that she was late. The haddock, trying to rub out the dirty spots on his skin, was also late. The mackerel went and put beautiful stripes on himself – pink and green and gold and all the colours of the sea and the sky. He made himself look so different that the other fish didn't know him and would have nothing to do with him. The skate came late as he had to swim all the way up from the sea bed.

While all these fish were trying to make themselves more beautiful and squabbling together, the shoals of herring twisted this way and that way in the turning tide. Time was up. The rising sun shone down and placed a sparkling crown above where the silver darlings swam, just beneath the surface of the sea. The herring were crowned by the sun and judged to be the most beautiful and speediest fish.

It's true when you look closely at a herring you can see the head is moulded into the body and the snout cuts through the water. The fins fit closely, and the eyes don't protrude. It has a smooth surface, and its forked tail helps it swim for long periods of time at high speed. In comparison, other fish are slow swimmers. The underside of the herring is silvery white, while its back is steely blue and black. When hungry birds look down, the metallic colours of the herring merge into the tones of the sea. Looked at from below by larger fish looking for prey, the silvery white of the belly makes

the herring look invisible against a light sky. So, you see, its beautiful colouring is really a protection against its enemies from the air above and from the water beneath. No wonder it's called King of the Sea.

We all loved herring and we knew they were good for us. Another great thing is that when herring are cheapest, they are at their best because they only come together in shoals (that means lots swimming together) when they're in tip-top condition. That's when the fishermen go out with their huge nets to catch them. They're caught at night and landed in the morning. So, you see, the herring really is the freshest fish you can buy.

I went back to see Peggy and told her the story of the King of the Sea. Peggy said, 'I'd better eat more herring then and I'll soon be as fit as a fiddle.' Peggy did get better and we enjoyed many tasty fish suppers together.

*Of all the fish that are in the sea, the herring is the one for me.*

# 8

# GREENLAND ON THE THAMES

If you take a boat for about a mile downriver from the famous Tower Bridge, you'll come to Rotherhithe. This is where Noah lived with his mum and dad, and he really knew all about where his family had lived for hundreds of years. He knew that Rotherhithe was the place where the Anglo-Saxons landed their cattle and where King Edward III had a palace in the year 1300 and something. He also knew that, for hundreds of years people had built ships here, fished in the river and sailed to distant lands. Others worked for many hours on the docks, unloading all the valuable cargoes from around the world.

But what he didn't know so much about was Rotherhithe's connection with the whaling industry.

Noah loved the magnificent, mysterious creatures that are whales. If you asked him about the humpback, the minke or the blue whale, he could tell you all about the differences between them. He knew that, for a long time, whales had really suffered badly and, in the last century, millions of them had been hunted and killed. But he also knew that now people wanted to protect whales.

He wanted to look after whales too because they are such amazing creatures. Whales are very clever, they can send messages to each other for miles across the ocean by making really beautiful, unusual-sounding songs. It's like nothing you've ever heard. It's their way of speaking to each other over such very long distances. They are impressive, intelligent and, to him, just lovely giant and gentle creatures who need our protection.

Today he was reading that, by looking after whales, we'll actually protect the planet.

Wow, this was new to him! He read that they help the atmosphere, just as much as the Amazon forests do, by filtering the poisons in the air, and this makes the world a healthier place.

While he was learning all this new information, his father was on the computer finding out about their family's history. He was checking the records of what his great-great-great grandfather was called and what he did for work. Suddenly his dad started singing ... about whales! But Noah wasn't so sure he liked the words of this song:

I'm bound off for Greenland
And ready to sail
In hopes to find riches
In hunting the whale …

Our ship is well rigged
And she's ready to sail
The crew they are anxious
To follow the whale

Where the icebergs do float
And the stormy winds blow
Where the land and the ocean
Are covered with snow

The cold coast of Greenland
Is barren and bare
No seed time nor harvest
Is ever known there

And the birds here sing sweetly
In mountain and dale
But there's no bird in Greenland
To sing to the whale

Noah was shocked, 'Dad, why are you singing that song? You shouldn't be singing songs about hunting whales!'

His father said, 'Oh, I know what you mean, Noah. These days we don't hunt whales, we look after them. But when I was young, this old folk song became popular again and, because of what I was reading just now, I suddenly remembered my dad singing it. You see, our family has lived in Rotherhithe for hundreds of years and I've been trying to find out about our ancestors. I've been checking the records at St Mary's church and most of

our ancestors worked on the river. They built ships, they were fishermen on the Thames and, whether we like it or not, they would most likely have sailed to the cold Arctic Ocean to hunt whales. It was dangerous work, but it was the work that so many people of the Thames did.

'But that's terrible, Dad, why didn't they want to protect the whales?'

Noah's dad suggested they go for a walk and, not very far from home, they came to Greenland Dock. Here there are now nice houses and apartments on the banks of a big stretch of water with a boat marina at one end. But it wasn't always like that. He started telling Noah all about the area, 'I know you love whales, I do too, and I really want to look after them just as you do. But life today isn't the life our ancestors lived. This place got its name because ships went out from here to the Arctic Ocean around Greenland, that huge island covered in glaciers that I sing about in the song. When they came back, they brought whale blubber, which they turned into oil.'

'Whale blubber?'

'Yes. It's a thick layer of fat under the skin of the whale that keeps them warm enough to swim in the icy water. Greenland was the place where most of the whales could be found and it's the place where the Inuit people still live. You see, a long time ago people just *had* to hunt whales. All the people who live in the Arctic have never had crops like barley or wheat to make bread and they didn't have vegetables or animals, like cows and sheep, so everything they ate had to come from the sea. Otherwise, they would've died.

'So, they had to hunt seals and whales to give them strength and keep them alive. But, like hunting peoples all over the world, they weren't greedy, they only took what they needed for themselves and nothing more. Nearly every part of the whale was used. They ate the meat, the skin, the blubber and the organs as well. They'd get all the vitamins, minerals, protein and fats that everyone needs to be healthy. They made baskets and fishing nets from the long bristle-like stuff in the whales' mouths called baleen and they used the bones to make tools and to carve masks for their ceremonies. Nothing at all was wasted.'

'Oh, I see,' said Noah. 'But wait a minute, *we* had crops for our wheat and vegetables and cows and sheep and orchards to grow fruit and stuff, so why did *we* have to hunt whales?'

'Well, in the old days we didn't have petrol or oil for the fuel that we know today. Rubber and plastic hadn't been invented and steel was very expensive and hard to make. Two hundred years ago, people didn't have all the things that make our lives easy today. Where would we be today without steel or petrol? So, people had to find other things – and whales provided those things that made life as easy as it is for us today.

'At night people had only candles to light their homes with, but whale oil meant that you could have bright oil lamps to read or work by at night. Then there was street lighting. The streets were pretty dim until whale oil made London the best-lit city in the world. All the newly invented machines – like spinning and weaving machines, steam engines, locomotives and the first typewriters – all needed this whale oil to keep them working smoothly. Baleen, hanging in long strips instead of teeth in the whales' mouths, was bendy and very strong and so it could be used to make umbrellas, chimney sweep brushes and hoops for the big crinoline dresses that women liked wearing. It was even used in their corsets to make them look slim. The oil also made soap and margarine to spread on bread and to cook with, because butter was too expensive for most ordinary people.

'So, because there were so many whales in the oceans, people thought it was all right to hunt them, just like people think it's all right to take fish from the ocean to eat. They were the answer to all the things that were needed to make people's lives better. But now we have all of these things from different sources and so we don't need to hunt whales. We need to protect them, just like you want to do. But your great-great-great-great grandfather was a whaler who sailed the cold, icy and dangerous waters of the Arctic like so many Rotherhithe men, so that he could feed his family.'

Noah was understanding that life two hundred years ago was very different from our lives and that his family too had been part of the Rotherhithe whaling trade. Here he was, just around the corner from where those sailing ships sailed from Greenland Dock, down the Thames to the sea and out to the lands of the frozen north.

He started to find out more and more. He read that the Inuit of Greenland really got to know and work with the whalers. Often, they helped to guide the ships, worked alongside the sailors and traded meat and salmon with the men on the ships for wooden and metal tools. The Inuit women would sew wonderful warm parka jackets made of fur for the sailors. They were much warmer than their own English woollen coats.

Some of the sailors learned the language and even had families in Greenland whom they only saw in the Arctic summer when they could hunt for the whales. Noah wondered if they'd tell stories to each other at night around the fire, or in the ship's hold, where the families stayed while working. Did his own whaling ancestors hear these stories and share their stories of London and the river?

Noah asked his dad to look out for books of Arctic and Inuit stories and one of his favourites was this one:

One day, an old woman was walking by the sea a little way from her village, in the cold land of Greenland. There was still ice on the water because, although it was spring and the ice was starting to break up, it took a long time for all the sea ice to melt away completely.

Just then, as she walked a bit further along the cold coast, she noticed a tiny polar bear on a piece of ice by the beach. The little bear was all on its own. 'Oh', she thought, 'somebody must have killed its mother and the dear little thing has no one to look after him.'

As she got closer, she saw it was looking at her with its big eyes that seemed to say, 'Please help me'. Without thinking, she went up to him and put her nose to his. This is what Inuit mothers do to their children to show them their love. And it's also what adults do when they meet a close friend. This greeting is called a *Kunik*. As she did so, she said, '*Kunik*', and this became his name. She said she'd look after him and he could become her son.

They went back to the village and became mother and son. She was happy because until now she'd had no husband or sons to hunt and fish for her and even though her neighbours shared their food with her, she had been lonely. Kunik was happy too because he now had a mother who loved him. Kunik was very popular with everyone, especially the children. He was very gentle with them and they loved to play with him. They slid and jumped and rolled in the snow and had so much fun. What a great thing to have your own little polar bear friend to play with!

They showed him how they went fishing and he soon learned to catch fish himself. He brought plenty of tasty things for his mother to eat and she was always glad of this. He became the best fisherman in the village. And even though he shared all that he caught with everyone, the other fishermen started to talk and complain, 'He catches more fish than we do, he's making it seem as though we're no good. Maybe it's time that we got rid of him. We'll have to kill him.'

But as they were saying all this, one of the children overheard and rushed to tell the old woman. When Kunik came back from hunting she had to tell him, 'You must leave the village, Kunik, they're plotting to kill you. Go away, but don't go so far away that I won't be able to find you.'

With tears in their eyes, Kunik, the polar bear, and his mother said goodbye. He looked back at her one last time, as he disappeared into the white distance.

She was now lonely once again and the children were sad to have lost their friend. She became thinner as she wasn't getting so much food.

That winter was a hard one for her. She sat alone in her little igloo as the cold blizzards blew outside. Then, one day in the spring she went walking by the seashore and walked further than she normally did, when, in the distance, she saw a white shape at the other end of the beach. The shape started to get closer. It was Kunik! He was running towards her!

When they came together, they put their noses together in the way they always did. But Kunik looked at his mother and saw she was so thin. She wasn't eating properly! He decided then that he would come there every day and bring lots of lovely food for her. And that's what happened. The old woman would regularly walk along the beach and Kunik would bring her the best fish and meat to eat.

All the people in the village understood what was happening, but they didn't mind. They knew that a polar bear just can't live in a village with ordinary people. But they also understood the old woman and Kunik truly loved each other and that was really important to each of them. They were left in peace, to meet out on the ice away from the village, whenever they wanted to. That was just as it should be. The people of the village continued to tell the story of this special love between an old woman and a polar bear, and that story has survived right up to our own day.

Noah came to understand that our lives, in our own day, are so much easier than they were for our ancestors. The Inuit people, the people of that village in Greenland, and Kunik himself, had to hunt to stay alive. The people of Rotherhithe also had to feed their families. They had to work by shipbuilding, unloading the ships at the docks and hunting whales in the Arctic. That was how they kept their own families alive in those hard days.

But now there is no need to hunt and kill these gigantic but gentle creatures. Noah decided he'd do something to help the whales to stay alive. Together with his friends at school they each collected a few coins from their spending money and with the help of their teachers and other classes in their school they joined the 'Adopt a Whale' scheme of the charity 'Whale and Dolphin Conservation'. Noah was keeping alive Rotherhithe's long tradition of connections with Greenland, the Arctic and the mighty and beautiful whales of the deep seas.

# SAILOR TALK

If you were a sailor on the river and the seas,
You'd need to understand words like these:
*Do you know the ropes?*
*Mind your Ps and Qs,*
Are you on *an even keel?*
I don't mean to confuse.

Well, *anchors aweigh,*
*As the crow flies,*
*At a rate of knots,*
Watch out, don't *capsize.*

Well done, *all sewn up*
You're *a leading light*
You can *flake out* now
It's the middle of the night.

Time to *pipe down*
The ship's *chock-a-block*,
We're sailing to the land of Nod
It's past twelve o'clock.

# 9

# FROM RIVERBED TO BARGE

Hello, my name is Jim and I'm a mudlark. They call us 'mudlarks' but it's no larking matter. It's how I earn my keep. We search in the mud of the Thames: once the tide is out, we step into the thick mud on the river's foreshore. We use our fingers and toes to search for anything that might have been dropped from ships – scraps of rope, coal, wood, iron and copper – anything that will sell. Sometimes we find old bones and we can sell them to factories that make soap.

It's 1870 and I live in Deptford, but in the summertime, when the tide is low, I make my way to Greenwich and we boys get busy in the mud below the windows of The Trafalgar and The Ship. Both of these are fine places where ladies and gentlemen come to eat and drink and be merry. They come to eat the famous 'whitebait'. Whitebait is a mixture of little fish, young herring and sprats, and very tasty. Even the members of the Houses of Parliament come down in a pleasure steamer to eat the famous Greenwich whitebait.

We can tell when the gentlemen get all flushed with wine because they get louder and laugh a lot and the sound of their voices

from the open windows comes down to us. Well, then we get very busy ourselves and sing a few snatches of song so that they'll notice us. Then they look out and dig into their pockets for their loose change and they fling the copper pennies they don't want out onto the mud. They like to see us scramble for them. We put on a bit of a show to keep them watching and digging into their pockets for more pennies.

We do well on fine summer evenings when the tide is low. What's not good are the winter nights when the tide is high and the fog is over the river. The water is busy with ships and they sound the foghorns to make sure they're noticed and not bumped into. The barges carrying hay and straw or stone and grain are the ones to avoid. They're so huge and heavy. They carry a little lantern in front, but the mist and fog can be so thick you don't see it until the barge is really close.

I have a friend, Harry, who works with his dad on a barge. I envy him. He has a proper job and even so there are times when he's left hungry, when his dad can't find a load to carry on his barge. At least he is snug and warm on board, just him and his dad. Whereas where I live, the wind, the damp river air and the fog creep in through the two small panes of broken glass, even though mother has tried to stuff the cracks with rags.

In the two rooms we live in, you can't move an elbow without hitting the wall or the table or a sister or brother and the soot from the fireplace smears the walls. I prefer to stay outside, and in the warm weather that's what I do. I sleep under the railway arches or find a rowboat that's moored up and crawl into it, though I have to be out quick as soon as it is daylight.

The River Thames is like a mother and father to me. I've come to know the river. I know from the colour of the sky at dawn and the cries of the birds what kind of day it will be. I love the wide, pale light before most people are up and about. I'd love nothing more than to be a waterman, own my own wherry and take passengers to and fro across the river. But that's not likely to be as I've no one to speak for me and I'd have to be apprenticed to a waterman for seven years and have enough money to buy my own wherry.

Second best would to be work on a barge. Ah well, 'If wishes were horses, then beggars would ride', as my dad says. I have to go home tonight as the clouds are gathering and soon it will rain heavily.

That night, as usual, I slept top to tail with my two younger brothers. Sure enough, when I woke in the early hours, the rain was pelting down and blowing in through the cracks in the windowpanes. Just then, there was a hammering on the door. Dad opened it and Bert, my friend's dad, was standing there, dripping wet. 'Is your boy Jim here?' he asked.

'I'm here,' I said. 'What's wrong, is Harry OK?'

'Harry's fine, it's my mate Joe, his boy has been taken ill with the fever and he has a load of coal to get up the river. The tide waits for no one and if he misses the flood-tide he'll have to wait twelve hours until he can shift it and that'll be too late. Harry says you've always wanted to work on the river. Here's your chance, boy. Help my friend and I'll do my best to get you a permanent place.'

I jumped out of bed. Dad gave me a slice of bread and then on with my trousers and jacket and out of the door with Harry's dad.

Life is like the river. Unpredictable. You never know when your luck will change.

★★★

That was seventy years ago. Jim was my dad and that was how he first started to work on the barges. I loved to hear his stories about those old barges that had once beaten their way up and down the east coast and the channel ports. Now they grumble and heave at their cables. Just like my old dad. When he left mudlarking, he was nine years old. Joe was the man he worked for, and he became like a second father to him.

Joe was born in Silvertown and could hear the sounds coming from the old boatbuilders' yards. At night he didn't fall asleep to the sound of leaves rustling in a night breeze or birds singing their last songs of the day, as I do, but to the sound of the heavy barges banging into each other at their moorings. He loved his life. He loved the river and knew it in all its different moods. After my dad left mudlarking, when he wasn't on the barge he stayed with Joe in Silvertown.

Being on the barge was hard work and my dad was good at it. He was able to leap from the shore to the barge, keep his balance and, when it was necessary, walk the length of the barge to fasten a tarpaulin, even when it was in choppy waters.

The barges had flat bottoms so they could skim across the mud of the river in very little water at low tide. Dad told me there was one time he fell off the barge, but it was in such shallow water he didn't have to swim after it, he ran through the mud and water and clambered back on board.

But when he got old, he was a heap of joints and not one of them worked. Pains in his knees, elbows, wrists, ankles and especially his knuckles. But he still told me stories of when he felt as free as a bird sailing up and down the river.

The barge Joe owned was called a 'stumpie'. This was because it didn't have a top sail. It carried whatever loads were in demand: often that was bricks from the famous brickfields in north Kent. They were yellow bricks, and they can be seen in many London houses from the nineteenth century. Even Downing Street, where the Prime Minister lives, is built from those yellow bricks.

Sometimes he took a barge full of horse dung down into the Kent countryside and maybe came back with the barge piled high with hay for the horses that pulled all the carts and carriages in London. My dad used to sit on top of a stack of hay piled ten feet above the deck and he'd have to shout out to Joe, who was steering, to warn him if there was another barge or boat coming towards them. They used to carry any cargo they could: flour, grain, coal, timber – anything.

Sometimes, though, there was no work and dad told me of one terrible time. This was his story:

It was November 1908. The weather had been terrible, fog everywhere for a whole week of days and nights. Joe's barge was tied up to buoys in the river at Woolwich. It was for a reason they were called 'starvation buoys'. He told me that at least they were lucky to be tied up and not drifting in the fog.

He and Joe had been ready to sail down into Kent to pick up a cargo of coal when the fog fell. It came in the early hours like a thick, wet blanket. Fog up the river, fog down the river, fog in the rigging of the great ships, fog hiding the barges and the small boats, fog rolling into the wharves and into the alleyways. Fog in their eyes and in their throats and they only had enough food and drink on board to last one day, enough for the trip there and back and no way to get to shore.

I have never been hungry. My dad had often been hungry, but never as hungry as that terrible week in November. 'Dad what did you do?' I asked.

Dad told me that the hunger was bad, but as time went on the hunger wasn't the worst of it. It was not knowing whether it was night or day, and he began to see things that weren't there and hear voices that didn't sound like they came from his time and place. He didn't know what was real and what wasn't or whether he was awake or dreaming.

I asked him what they had to eat. He told me they had something and they made it last. They had two small onions, which they ate raw with a rind of cheese and a hunk of bread. They had water and, luckily, they had some dog biscuits in a jar they were saving as a special treat for Joe's old mutt, Spot. They were in the shape of a bone and were made from milk, minerals and meat products. I was amazed that they ate dog biscuits, but my dad told me they were glad to have them. Joe put them in a pan with some water and mushed them up, added a bit of onion and made a kind of pancake with them. They were lucky enough to have a few lumps of coal left from the last trip down into Kent so they could have a small fire in the stove to cook by. Also, for as long as it lasted, they had a warm glow to cheer them up.

But my dad told me he didn't know if he had a fever or whether what he was hearing on the river really happened. He heard banging and clanging. He smelt smoke from burning torches, he heard sounds as though there was a war, shouting and drums. Then a chorus of voices came out of the fog:

'Come all you Vulcans, stout and strong
Unto St Clem we do belong.'

And then:

'I am the real St Clement,
the first founder of brass, iron and steel
– from the ore.

I have been to Mount Etna,
where the God Vulcan first built his forge
and forged the armour and thunderbolts
for the God Jupiter.'

He said he didn't tell anyone about it for a long time in case they thought he was crazy, but then he found out that what he'd heard were the foundry workers, blacksmiths, seamen and their apprentices celebrating the feast of St Clement.

Of course, it was 23 November, the eve of the feast of St Clement, the saint that seamen claim as their patron saint. All the apprentices dressed up and had a big parade, making a huge noise with tongs and shovels and wooden hammers and sledgehammers. They paraded around the town, stopping at every public house, collecting money. It was called 'Old Clem's night' and it started with a bang and a shower of sparks.

I told dad he must tell me more stories from when he was young. I really wanted to know them. Dad did tell me more stories of his life on the river and that was more than forty years ago. I am a dad and a grandad myself now and I tell these stories to my children and grandchildren. Stories from a time that is now so different to the times we live in.

You ask your mums and dads for their stories. A family needs its stories.

# THE RIVERBED

Gulls in bib and tucker and pert pintails
line up for lunch and perch on rails.
Sharp-beaked gulls with sharper cries
are descending from the skies.

While down below
mud, stick and stone,
pot, nail and bone
of the riverbed.

Fishermen sit on the banks of the river.
Cormorants catch eels all a-quiver.
Tugs pull barges wide.
Herons fish at the edge of the tide.

While down below,
mud, stick and stone,
pot, nail and bone
of the riverbed.

# 10

# FERRIES AND FISHES

Albert loved it when his father told him stories. He told him old tales of dragons and heroes and battles at sea and sometimes there were stories that would make him feel cosy and sleepy. He also told him how he'd first arrived in London on a ship from China, how he'd been a sailor on ships that brought tea, silk and lovely fine pottery to London and how, while he was waiting for a job on a ship returning to China, he had met Albert's mum near the docks as she got off the ferry from Rotherhithe. They got married, settled near the docks at Limehouse and together set up a business washing other people's clothes.

Albert's mother had grown up on the other side of the river at Bermondsey and knew lots

of people who needed their clothes washing. The dirty clothes had to be brought across the river every day to be washed, then returned clean in the next few days. The time came when his mum and dad thought Albert was old enough to go on the ferry each day to collect the clothes and return them back to Bermondsey when they'd been washed. Their laundry was getting busier all the time and now that Albert was able to do this, mum could spend more time with dad doing the extra work at the laundry.

Sometimes, when they got a little break, Albert's dad would start a story, which Albert was always eager to hear. One day, he told him a story in which the main character had Albert's name. That was a brilliant way to start and Albert would listen with 'wide open ears', as his father used to joke, when he really liked a story:

A long time ago, there lived a young man in a little house by the river. His name was Albert and he lived with his elderly mother and took such good care of her that everyone knew him for his kindness and the love he showed.

His mother had been sick in bed for a long time. It was winter, it was very cold, and he made sure she was wrapped up warm. But he couldn't get her to eat anything and he'd often say, 'Oh come on, dear mother, please try to eat something. You need to eat to get strong and to get better.'

'I know,' she would say, 'but I just don't feel like eating. I've got no appetite.'

'But maybe there is something special that I could get that would make you want to eat – something that would get your appetite working again.'

'Well,' she said, 'I do like fish, and my favourite fish is carp. Perhaps it would … but, no it's winter time and …'

Before she'd finished speaking Albert said, 'Yes! That's it. I'll go and find some!'

The fish market was on the other side of the river and you had to take a ferry to get across. He ran quickly down to the river and got onto the ferry that was waiting for passengers. When the boat reached the middle of the river, a huge shiny fish jumped up into the air out of the water and landed, plop! onto the bottom of the ferry.

'Well, I never!' said the waterman. 'That's never happened to me in all the years I've been ferrying people across this river.'

'Oh,' said Albert, amazed, 'I'm just on my way to buy a carp for my mother at the market. Would you mind selling it to me?'

'No, no way, lad. I've never had a fish jumping into my boat before. That's going to bring me luck, that is.'

Albert went to the market hoping he'd be able to get a carp for his mum. But when he got there every stallholder laughed at him and told him the same thing, 'You can't get carp in winter. You just don't see them anywhere. They wait until it gets warmer before swimming up and down the river. Have you never heard that?'

Albert was so sad. Was there anything else his mother liked that he could get in wintertime? If she didn't eat anything she might get so sick that she would die. He didn't know what to do, so just for now, he thought he would go home to be with her.

Back on the ferry, once it was out in the middle of the river there was a bright flash and a sudden movement to one side of the boat. It was something shiny jumping out of the water and landing, plop! onto the bottom of the ferry.

'What … another carp?' said the waterman. 'Well I'll be. I've never had a … wait a minute, wasn't it you who was in the boat before, when the other carp landed here?'

'Yes sir, it was.'

'And didn't you say you wanted to buy a carp?'

'I did sir, though everyone tells me that you can't find carp in winter. But you see, my mother is very sick, and the only thing she wants to eat is carp.'

'Well glory be. Heaven must have sent us a miracle today. I've never seen a carp in winter but today I've seen two and right here on my ferry! Here boy, take them home to your Mum.'

'But won't you keep one, sir?'

'No, boy, you're a good lad and you should have them both. If they help your mother get well again, I'd be very happy.'

Back home, Albert cooked the carp and the smell of the fish made his mother start to sit up straight away. She tried a little, smiled and then asked for some more. Over the next few days, she grew stronger and stronger until she was strong enough to ask Albert to take her down to the river to thank the waterman for his kindness.

The winter passed and for many more years Albert and his mother would cross the river by ferry to the fish market on the other side.

Albert loved this story and, after hearing it, he started seeing fish jumping out of the water as he crossed over on his errands to Bermondsey. He wanted to know if this was a story from China or from England.

But Albert's father looked at him and answered, 'Well where *do* stories come from? Stories, just like people, travel from place to place. They cross borders, they travel the seas, they sail up rivers. They go from one person's mouth to another person's ears, and they have to be told to stay alive. I'll leave you to decide where this story comes from. But tell me Albert, what about you? Do you think you're English or do you think you're Chinese?'

'Well, Dad, you're Chinese and Mum is English so I suppose that would make me, er … er … a Londoner!'

This made mum and dad smile because they agreed. 'Yes, Albert, you're a Londoner and we're both Londoners too.'

*Thames Fishing – a little note: For thousands of years, fish from the Thames provided healthy food for the people of London. Many families who lived right on the shore would earn their living by selling fish. A father would train his son for about seven years, starting at the age of nine. After this apprenticeship, the boy would be a fully trained Thames fisherman. Later, when he became a father, he would go out, perhaps with his son, in a 'peterboat', which had a well in it for holding live fish and the space for just one man and a boy. The popular fish were eels, seabass, flounder, smelt, dover sole and of course, as in China, carp.*

*Thames Ferries – a little note: For hundreds of years London had two big problems. Number one, terrible roads and number two, only one narrow and crowded bridge across the Thames: London Bridge, first built by the Romans. Now there are thirty-five bridges, from Hampton Court Bridge, by the Tudor royal palace, to the famous Tower Bridge, more than twenty miles downstream and pictured on the cover of this book.*

*Because there was just one narrow bridge, the quickest and easiest way to cross, or travel up and down the river, was by ferry. In olden days, they were called wherries and rowed by a waterman. The Thames was like London's superhighway and there were thousands of wherries crossing at every part of the river.*

*There were steps leading down to where you could hire a 'long ferry' to take you along the river, such as from Westminster to Billingsgate, or you could hire a wherry to take you across from the city to Southwark on the south bank, where you could see plays by Shakespeare at the famous Globe or Rose Theatre.*

*The men who worked a wherry, a ferry or a barge often learned the job from their fathers and grandfathers and they had to know about all the tides and currents in the often dangerous Thames to make sure that passengers were able to cross safely.*

# A BOAT BY ANY OTHER NAME

Barges, cruisers, houseboats,
all of these are afloat
on the Thames for you to see.
How many more can there be?

Canoes and kayaks by the score,
rowing boats and some more.
River police and fireboats too,
paddle steamers, there are a few.

Viking longboats have been found
in the mud, not underground.
Currachs, shallops, narrowboats;
the last of these are still afloat.

Trawlers, cutters, skiffs and clippers,
tall ships and square riggers.
The Thames will take you out to sea.
On which boat would you like to be?

# 11

# THE WHALE ROAD

We had come far. My name is Olaf, and I am a young man and have not yet spilt blood, nor do I want to. Yet I am here, out on the North Sea and about to enter the river that will lead us to the place they call *Lundenwic*.

We call the sea 'the Old Grey Widow Maker' and, yes, we have lost men on this voyage. It was hard going, and my stomach is empty and my bones ache. The dragon's head is up to its neck in foam. This is the salt spray, the deep way, hands blistered, and muscles torn. The rhythm of our oars tames the sea and even the mighty waves that erode the rocks and turn pebbles to sand.

The whale road
The grey road
The dragon's prow
Up to its neck in foam.

The salt spray
The deep way
Backs turned
Away from home.

The swift glide
Down the wave's side
The wind's scream
The hail-stone.

The blind night
No star in sight
Cursed to heave
And blindly roam.

Our land is small
On us it falls
To ride and conquer
The raging combs.

Heave Viking men, bend your backs, chase the storm.

There is no stopping until we find land. It is there before us, huddled and dark in the swirling grey mist that will hide us from those who are not pleased to see us coming. They will hide or they will run, or they may fight. I am tired and want none of it. There is no choice.

We haul the boat up onto the muddy shore. A bird calls – or is it a warning call from the throat of a man, imitating a bird?

My father was a warrior and he died in battle. We were able to bury him with full honours. He was a brave warrior and his soul will survive to go on living in the next world. We buried him with all kinds of things he might need: clothes and weapons.

I am not like my father. I would like to settle down on land. I would like to farm this land that we've reached.

All is quiet. We are on a bend of the River *Tamyse*. We are going to make camp and I and some other younger men will wait here on the hill above the place known as *Grenawic* village with some of our ships. The more experienced warriors have gone on into Kent along the high ground to the south, along the old road that leads to Canterbury. There is sure to be fighting and bloodshed there. I am glad I am not with them.

It is quiet here. *Grenawic* is a small fishing village with some small fishing boats harboured there and safe anchorage for our ships. I wish to get along with the people here. I have a plan that I am not sharing with anyone. I do not want to go back to sea. I do not want to fight and kill and steal. I want to stay in this pleasant, green place. I could disappear into the countryside.

I volunteered to go down into the fishing village and barter for some things we need. We have some *danegeld* here and I will get flour and meat. We can catch plenty of fish. From a little way off I see an older man trying to step from his boat onto land, but he slips and falls into the water. He is in some difficulty. I run as fast as I can and help him onto shore.

He is frightened of me at first. I speak to him in his own language. I know a little. It is not so different form my own language, Norse. '*Heill ok saell,*' I say as a greeting. He is surprised, he is grateful. He leads me to his small cottage and sits me down. He talks for a long while. I begin to understand what he is telling me. He had a son but that one son drowned. He is on his own. He has no one to help him go fishing or mend his boat. I tell him, 'I will come down to help you whenever I can.' He is pleased.

I go back up the hill to the camp and say nothing to the other men about what has happened. Days turn to weeks, weeks to months, and still the older men have not returned from Canterbury. I am glad. I am getting to know this old man very well. He has become a little like a father to me and I think, that for him, I am becoming another son.

One day, he tells me that he would like to leave *Grenawic* and go further downriver. He says it is quieter there and there is land that his family has lived on for many generations. He asks me if I will go with him. I do not have to think about this. It is what I hoped for. I speak his language very well now.

I want to live in peace. I want to live on land and catch fish from the beautiful river. I would not care if I never saw the North Sea again.

He takes a week to prepare and then we are leaving early on the last day of August 1011.

★★★

Time passed and then I had friends among these people. I was young and strong and they were glad of my help. I had my own small cottage. I had land where I could grow food and a fish-full river.

Stories and news travelled from *Grenawic*. I heard that the older warriors had returned from Canterbury, and they had brought the Archbishop Alphege with them and were asking for a ransom of three thousand pieces of silver. But the archbishop would not accept this. He would rather lay down his life than make the people poor by giving the Viking warriors so much money.

Sadly, that is what happened. He did lose his life and I am glad I was not part of it. I want no part in spilling any man's blood. I want to live in peace in this small settlement by the *Tamyse*.

We Vikings have a saying, 'There is a time for everything'. This is now my time and how I want to live. Also, I know there are many Vikings like me who want to settle down in this green land. I am sure in generations to come there will be many families who have Viking ancestors and there will be many words in the language they speak that will come from Norse, the language we brought to these shores.

I wish you well, all of you who will come after me, coming from many lands, and just as the waters of the oceans and the flowing rivers, arriving here.

# OLD NORSE

*A little note:* Here are just some of the old Norse words that are still alive and kicking in the English language:

*Dirt*, *muck* and *mire*,
You are speaking like a Viking.
*Ransack* and *slaughter*,
Just the same.

If I bring you *tidings*,
You are speaking like a Viking.
*Club*, *bug* and *blunder*,
Just the same.

*Sky*, *skip* and *billow*,
You are speaking like a Viking.
*Freckles* and *glitter*,
Just the same.

*Whisk*, *scale* and *scrape*
You are speaking like a Viking,
*Dregs*, *eggs* and *legs*,
Just the same.

# OUR THANKS

We'd like to thank Dr Tom Bolton, author of *London's Lost Rivers* (Volume I and II), for his invaluable help and advice, and the volunteers at The Wandle Industrial Museum and at Merton Abbey Mills for their enthusiasm about London's smaller but hugely important working rivers.

We'd also like to thank Eric Huntley for his feedback on the opening story, *The Lion Keeper's Apprentice*.

The
History
Press

The destination for history
**www.thehistorypress.co.uk**